The Guardian of AURUM

A. J. Behul

ISBN: 978-1-61244-552-6
Library of Congress Control Number: 2017907328

Printed in the United States of America

Halo Publishing International
1100 NW Loop 410
Suite 700 - 176
San Antonio, Texas 78213
Toll Free 1-877-705-9647
www.halopublishing.com
E-mail: contact@halopublishing.com

DEDICATED TO:

"Mis chicas"

My parents
(In the Great White North)

My Security Colleagues
(Who get up every day to protect and serve others, with no armor, super human powers or provenance from Krypton)

PROLOGUE

Rampant organized crime. Violence. Lawlessness. The fluctuating price of gold could bring the Company to its knees. Employee executions, kidnappings, extortion, and fraud are commonplace, with the internationally renowned case of forty-three missing students from Ayotzinapa at the doorstep to one of its mines.

Caught between the grip of the Company and Organized Crime, Aline soon finds herself in a downward spiral of conscience where the line between good and evil becomes more blurred with each passing day, transforming her from the holding of the Seraphim to the order of the Angelorum Lapsus. Will she be able to transcend the darkness and find light anew, or will she be sentenced to the Abyss for eternity?

Sunrise over mine,
Dark shadows fall onto light,
Seraphim align.

CHAPTER 1

Aline was jarred awake by the abrupt landing of the Company's King Air on the airstrip, about fifteen minutes from the mine. She was still a bit groggy from her catnap that began after takeoff from Toluca Airport in the State of Mexico.

"Please remain in your seats with your seat belts fastened until we come to a complete stop," announced the pilot. Exiting the aircraft, Aline squinted involuntarily, bringing up her left hand to shade her eyes from the hot desert sun. She picked up her backpack from the cargo hold and threw it over her shoulder, proceeding to the security checkpoint. The standard-issue, steel-toed safety boots felt heavy, and her new white hard hat, an unfamiliar additional weight on the top of her already moist forehead.

"Buenos días, señorita," said the security officer.

"Buenos días."

"May I check your bag, please?" As a well-seasoned security expert, Aline quickly took in her surroundings, including the blatantly obvious uniformed and heavily armed security personnel stationed around the airfield and the 4x4 pickups with polarized windows and flashing LED light bars.

Nice welcome, she thought.

Driving to the mine was something new for Aline. Arid desert as far as the eye could see—cactus and agaves, tumbleweed, and the occasional roadrunner, or *correcaminos*, darting across the road. Traditional Mexican *banda* music played on the radio in the background while one of her bosses—the director of Corporate Security, compatriot, and ex-Mountie Mr. Straddler—sat behind her, filling up a seat (and a half) with his bearlike stature. He made small talk about the particularities of the region while reminiscing about law enforcement days. The SUV sped along, leaving a trail of dust in its wake, with no hopes of a Starbucks popping up anytime soon.

Second security checkpoint. Two officers with assault rifles trying to shelter themselves from the incessant sun, heat, and dust under a makeshift, open-concept guardhouse made of discarded metal and aluminum sheet roofing. The futility of their efforts was evident in their flushed faces and clammy, stained uniforms. The sight of the weapons elicited an automatic response; Aline pressed her left forearm against her side, looking for the concealed Glock 25 she had been accustomed to carrying during EP, or executive protection assignments, only to find nothing.

The mine was big. Really big. The largest open-pit gold mine in Mexico with operations on a site of two thousand hectares, producing an average of six hundred thousand ounces of Au per year.[1] The vehicle

••••••••••••••••••

1 Au—The symbol for the chemical element gold, from the Latin word "aurum," meaning gold.

came to a stop in front of the administration building, and a brawny guy in khaki combat pants, hard hat, and fluorescent orange safety vest opened the side door. "We have a problem on our hands," he said. "A local group from the community is trying to take over the mine union and has started to form blockades at all entry points to the property."

"How long do you think this will last?" inquired Aline.

"Who knows? Hope you're ready to stay for a while."

Before she could get another word in, the head of site security dashed off, mumbling something about a meeting.

As the idea of spending a number of days with only one change of underwear and a toothbrush sank in, Aline instinctively formed an ad hoc contingency plan, evaluating how long the food, water, and diesel reserves would last, alternatives for medical evacuations, the continuity of production, and where to set up temporary safe houses in case management had to hole up somewhere. All the while, her boss, hands folded comfortably across his belly, picked up right where he had left off with his train of thought, seemingly oblivious to the clear and imminent crisis.

It took about two minutes for the adrenaline already racing through Aline's body to get the best of her, and she unexpectedly opened the door, cutting off the ongoing monologue mid-sentence with a curt, "Excuse me, I'll be right back," as she stepped out of the vehicle and headed for the main building.

"Buenos días," Aline said as she reached the reception desk. "I'm looking for the head of site security."

"And who's looking for him?" asked the receptionist smugly.

"Aline Belanger, Regional Director of Security. His new boss."

"Oh," she stammered sheepishly. "He's in the meeting room at the end of the hallway."

"Thank you," Aline replied as she sped down the corridor. Approaching the door, she knocked purposefully and entered the room, not waiting for a response. About twenty-five people looked at her, and the main speaker—the local human resources manager—stopped talking. The head of security was leaning lazily against a sidewall with his arms crossed.

"Excuse me. Aline Belanger, Regional Director of Security. Will anyone here be leaving on the flight scheduled to depart in thirty minutes?" The HR manager looked around and answered with a shake of his head while Aline, with eyebrows raised, pointed her index finger intently at the head of site security and changed it to an unmistakable gesture of, "Let's go. It's time to get the hell out of here."

Walking energetically toward the SUV, she turned to the security guy, who was now a bit more attentive and up to speed. "Are there any available 4x4's right now?"

"Yes. I can have one of my officers bring one down," he responded.

"Okay. How about the mine's exit points?"

"No, all of them are completely blocked."

"What about off-road?"

Her new charge was pensive. "Well, I guess we could cross a part of the desert."

"Fine," said Aline. "Make it happen."

Aline informed Mr. Straddler of the situation as the requested 4x4 drove up. Boarding the vehicle, they headed across bumpy terrain toward one of the farther perimeter fences of the mine's property. After about ten minutes, they reached the anticipated destination and quickly disembarked. No demonstrators in sight.

"What now?" asked Aline. The head of security and his 2 I/C, or second-in-command, made their way to one of the wooden posts that held the perimeter section together—which truthfully looked more like an improvised fence to enclose cattle than something that would effectively impede unauthorized trespassing—and pulled it out of the ground. Then they pulled out another post so there was enough of an opening for the pickup. After the truck passed over the downed fencing, they stopped and readjusted the posts to make it look like nothing had been altered.

After fifteen minutes, they reached the now-familiar airstrip. The aircraft was already lined up and ready for takeoff. Aline and her boss jumped out of the pickup, shook hands with the security guys, and said farewell, quickly heading toward the King Air.

"I'll check in with you when I get back to the office," she shouted at the security chief over the noise of the engine. As the plane taxied down the runway and became airborne, she looked through the window and quietly sighed with relief. Her first security experience in the Company's Zacatecas mine was in the books.

CHAPTER 2

Aline sipped her freshly brewed coffee and closed her eyes, taking in the aroma. She gazed out the window of her spacious new office on the fifteenth floor that overlooked Avenida Palmas, directly in front of the monumental church—Our Lady of Covadonga—and its captivating, neoclassical architecture. As it was still early morning, the city's smog had not yet reached its apex, and she could see the outline of the volcanoes Popocatepetl and Iztaccihuatl, the former still active, located some seventy kilometers southeast of Mexico City. Her business suit was smart, neatly pressed, and professional, only confirming the fact that she was a perfect fit for the corporate office. As she took another sip of java, her mind wandered back to the job interview that had taken place about three weeks ago.

"Ms. Belanger, please come in. I am the regional director of Human Resources, Mr. Johnnie. Let me introduce you to our senior vice president, Mr. Bozeman, and our director of Corporate Security, Mr. Straddler. Welcome to the largest gold-producing company in Mexico, and at present, the second-largest gold mining corporation in the world. Please tell us a little about yourself."

Aline Jean Belanger was a Canadian national, fitting as the Company was based in Vancouver, with an Eastern European background. She was born in an industrial port city on Lake Ontario about sixty-five kilometers west of Toronto. Her father had sought political asylum in Canada from the Communist regime a couple of years after her mother had crossed the ocean by boat with Aline's uncle and grandmother. Her parents had met at an ethnic community event, and roughly a year after her birth, they moved to Hogtown, where she was raised.[2]

Aline had always been fascinated by martial arts, with its discipline, honor, and techniques that enable a person to defend themselves and their loved ones from peril. That was Aline: Mother's little angel. Always guarding. Always protecting. Perhaps sent from the holding of the Seraphim, the first order of those who see most clearly and take human form, accepting a mortal existence in exchange for having no recollection or inkling of origin.

At the age of eleven, Aline began her journey in the combative arts, savoring the training and watching her belt colors change from white to brown. By the time she turned twenty, Aline had attained her black sash in Shaolin kung fu, the result of a three-day test in frigid March at a snow-covered, secluded retreat in northern Ontario. She had also become proficient with various oriental weaponry, including the balisong—a.k.a. the Filipino butterfly knife—and nunchakus. Many of her classmates in high school had been co-aficionados, so they all continuously trained and exchanged techniques.

Aline went on to the University of Toronto to pursue a bachelor's degree in political science. University

2 Hogtown—A historic Canadian nickname for the City of Toronto.

studies ran parallel to part-time jobs, intensive training, and certification in use of force, executive protection, pressure points, and tactical communication at Meaford and Fort York military bases. Her education was imparted by renowned instructors, including ex-SAS (Special Air Service) members, police officers from the U.K. and Canada who were former members of specialized tactical groups, and skilled experts in hand-to-hand combat.

At twenty-nine, Aline achieved her black belt 1st dan and title of sifu in a hybrid system made up of more than thirty-six styles and systems, including Muay Thai, Kali, Brazilian Jiu-Jitsu, Sambo (from Russia), and stick-fighting, not to mention meditation techniques, auto-suggestion, and NLP (neuro-linguistic programming).

In 1999, she headed south to Mexico where she picked up Spanish and then German a couple of years later when she was hired to lead the Security Department for a German automotive giant located in a quaint colonial city southeast of Mexico City. During that time, through one of her bosses, an ex-GSG 9 (Grenzschutzgruppe 9) member, she was able to take part in a rigorous, instructor-level firearms certification program in the Arizona desert that focused on executive protection.[3]

Cultural immersion aside, Aline needed to make money, and with her limited repertoire of Spanish — *hola, cerveza,* and *baño*—job prospects were few and far between. She made the acquaintance of a stocky

3 GSG 9—German counter-terrorism, hostage rescue, and the special operations police unit pertaining to the Federal Police.

Sicilian brawler and owner of a small pizza place. He reminded her of a tall action-movie star of the '80s with slicked hair tied back into a ponytail who punished his adversaries with wrist-snapping and bone-breaking twists and turns. Only this guy was about a foot shorter. He was mean and tough enough, though. After a while, he offered her a cash-paying job of collecting money from certain "clients" that were delinquent on loans.

"You wouldn't be expected to really hurt anyone," he said, trying to cajole her. "Just remind them that their payments are due."

"Um, no thanks," Aline retorted. She did, however, accept a couple of future assignments that he had set up to protect the juniors of Mexican businessmen.[4]

After six months, Aline was conversational in Spanish thanks to television, radio, and just expressing herself as best she could by interacting with people on a daily basis. One afternoon, as she was having a snack and flipping through TV channels, she stopped on a movie that seemed particularly familiar. "Wow!" she burst out as she watched herself on the screen in front of her. She had taken on a minor role in the film, which was shot in February just before she left Canada. A martial arts flick, she played one of four hired hit men in a barn scene, but she had never seen it. It wasn't a speaking part. She was only the victim of a Chinese star to the hand and a kick to the head from the main

....

4 Junior(s)—A colloquial term used in Mexico that refers to the male teenage children of wealthy families. Juniors have the notorious reputation of drinking to excess, gambling, soliciting the service of prostitutes, and generally behaving in an obnoxious, rude, and arrogant manner.

protagonist. Halfway through her tub of popcorn, she waited excitedly to see her name in the credit roll: *Aline Belanger–Gunman at Barn*. Satisfying, though she was quite sure that there wouldn't be any royalty checks anytime soon.

As her reputation grew, the executive protection and security jobs started rolling in—local government personalities, businessmen, and professional athletes. Aline was soon contracted to coordinate security for the Senior PGA Tour at La Vista Golf Club in Cholula, liaising with the event's American security counterpart, a retired FBI agent. She was responsible for coordinating one hundred seventeen officers from Auxiliary, Municipal, State, and Traffic police.

There was morning dew on the freshly cut green, and there was a chill in the air as she drove the designated *seguridad* golf cart at "full speed" toward the clubhouse. Earlier on, she had issued standing orders to the police officers who would be stationed at different points throughout the eighteen-hole course.

"Y por el amor de Dios, please remember that there will be many foreigners here for the first time in Mexico. Let's try to give them a good impression, okay?"

"Of course, señorita," said the *comandante* of the Auxiliary Police assuredly. He was responsible for ground operations at the club.

In the afternoon, Aline decided to drive through the entire course, just to make sure that everything was running smoothly. At the eighteenth hole, she "slammed" on the brakes and got out, approaching two police officers who were lying on the grass with their eyes closed.

"Tired, are we?" she asked, dismayed at their lack of professionalism and discipline.

"Es que…we worked a double shift yesterday and weren't able to sleep," they replied.

"No comment," she said, getting back into the cart and driving off to the main gate. The gig was short-lived, but it would get her needed exposure for future contracts in training law enforcement and private security personnel.

After the PGA contract, she enrolled herself in a five-day training course on police science and criminal investigation hosted at the convention center located downtown in the historic center of Puebla. It was a packed hall with about one hundred fifty *judiciales*.[5]

"¿Qué onda, güey?" asked a big, tanned guy with thick, dark moustache, open shirt, gold chains, and a pearl-handled pistol protruding from his belt.[6]

"Nada," Aline replied. It was about all that her extensive vocabulary would give her.

Stepping closer to join the conversation, the guy's sidekick, a pint-sized fellow with numerous gold rings who wore the archetypal black, gold-embroidered, *judiciales* jacket with the national Mexican eagle emblem and PJE designation on the back, smiled and asked, "*¿De* dónde vienes?"

"Canadá," she said.

5 *Judiciales*–Agents from the State Judicial Police (PJE), which is no longer in existence. The present organizational equivalent is the Ministerial Police, which is part of any given state's General Attorney's Office.

6 *¿Qué onda, güey?*–Slang phrase, basically meaning, "What's up, man?"

"Ah. Mucho frío."

"Sí." Aline sighed. *I won't hear that comment too often*, she thought sarcastically.

They exchanged contact information and went back into the training session.

On the third day, the general director of the event approached her during a break, inquiring as to who she was and why she was participating in the course.

"¿Y qué haces aquí?" he asked, befuddled at the fact that there was a foreigner—in a business suit no less—who had been sitting in the front row for the last couple of days among a mass of about two hundred pistol-toting, cowboy boot-wearing agents, including invited guests and VIPs from the military and law enforcement.

"Always learning something new," she said.

After chatting for a while about Aline's experience and training in Canada, he asked whether she could bring him her resume the next day. By the following weekend, she was sitting at a table with her name on a nameplate and a Canadian flag in front of her as a panel guest instructor at the same course in Mexico City.

Aline continued to train hard physically, running stairs in a neighborhood called La Paz, going to the gym, and keeping up her fighting skills. On a trip to Mexico City for an interview with a martial arts magazine, she made contact with an event promoter through whom she would eventually fight semi-pro in kickboxing, full contact, and MMA.[7]

"Just out of curiosity, do you have any hands-on business experience in Mexico?" probed Mr. Johnnie.

....

7 MMA—Mixed martial arts.

"Yes. Before I entered the automotive industry, I opened and managed two micro-companies: a security guard service provider and a self-defense institute open to the public."

During that time, Aline had also organized a very successful exhibition at a prestigious local university. Having been named on the instructor's list for the event, she led women's kickboxing classes. She later showcased her companies at security expos and conventions, in addition to giving TV and radio interviews on the topic of security.

"Well, I can see that you also completed an executive MBA at the Universidad de Las Américas, Puebla," continued the HR director.

"That's right. Specializing in finance," she added.

"That must have improved your business acumen significantly," interjected Mr. Bozeman, her future direct-line reporting boss.

"Absolutely," she said.

"What kind of security strategy would you propose for handling the complexities of mining in Mexico?" asked Mr. Straddler.

Having researched the Company beforehand—reading its latest annual report and monitoring gold prices and market capitalization in real time, along with the security climate in its areas of operation—Aline handed each of them a prepared hard copy of the data-driven strategy for all current Company operations in the region.

"In addition to mitigating risk and establishing adequate measures, we need to focus on intelligence-driven security that aligns with business objectives and adds value to the sustainability of the company," Aline replied.

A couple of hours later, the interview ended. She was hired.

****

Acapulco in August was hot, and the sea breeze did little more than move the humid air around. The virgin *piña colada* was refreshing and sort of made Aline feel as if she were on a weekend getaway, even though it was actually Monday afternoon and a work day.

"So, how do you like Acapulco?" asked Karmyn, the Company's event coordinator and part of the HR Department.

"Of course she likes it," interrupted Mr. Straddler. "Any reason that a Canadian gets to wear shorts is always received positively."

"That's right," laughed Aline.

On the agenda: preliminary security rounds and liaising with local contacts. She needed to establish event access control, review primary and secondary hotels, carry out route reconnaissance, and confirm the locations of hospitals and clinics for the upcoming mining convention in October. The biannual event was huge, drawing thousands of visitors, including hundreds of employees and their spouses from all of the Company's mine sites and offices in the Americas. The Pacific port had turned into the default venue for the convention, even though security concerns had increased significantly over the last few years due to incidents involving organized crime, which made Corporate uneasy.

"If you are in agreement, we can set up this parking bay to temporarily house the armored vehicles of our VIPs," said Aline to the hotel security manager. A number of top execs would be attending the event, and even though the Company was not big on high-level executive protection, certain measures were an absolute must.

"No problem," answered the security manager. "We can provide you with anything that you may require."

"Muchas gracias," said Aline.

In the meantime, the hotel valet brought up their rental car and handed her the keys while she gave him the ticket.

"Gracias," she said. The three of them got in and drove off to the convention center, the main site of the event. As they approached, they saw a sign in front:

CLOSED. UNDER CONSTRUCTION.

"Unbelievable," said Mr. Straddler. "The convention is coming up, and they're still building things?"

"Looks like it. Let me see what the actual situation is," said Aline, putting the vehicle into park. "Make sure you put on an important face," she said to her boss, winking.

She walked up to the door and knocked loudly.

"¿Sí, buenos *días*?" asked a guard sleepily.

"Buenos días. Could I please speak to the coordinator of the center?"

"May I ask who would like to speak to her?"

"Yes, of course. My name is Aline Belanger. I'm from the company that is the main sponsor for the upcoming mining convention. Do you see the man in the car behind me?" she asked, lowering her voice and pointing to Mr. Straddler, who was now sitting up and looking dignified.

"Yes. Who is he?" asked the guard curiously.

"Well, he's a very important person from the head office in Vancouver, Canada, and this is the only day that he is in Acapulco. Do you think that we could see the coordinator?"

"Por supuesto. Give me a moment, and I will inform her that you are here."

"Muchísimas gracias, señor."

Aline walked back to the car and got in while the guard radioed the administration office.

"What did you say to him?" asked Mr. Straddler.

"Oh, I said that you were a VIP from the head office inspecting the site."

"Good thinking," he said.

"Not bad," added Karmyn, smiling.

After a few moments, they were escorted in and provided hard hats. The coordinator welcomed them into the office wholeheartedly.

****

Aline was off to the mine located in the state of Guerrero. A week had passed since she had helped gain entry to the convention center in Acapulco, heading off a possible event disaster.

The early morning drive started from the corporate office. An hour and a half later, they reached Cuernavaca in the state of Morelos.

"Any chance of getting some grub?" Aline asked the company driver.

Quick to respond and practice his English, the driver said, "Yes, of course. There is a very famous roadside place on the way to the mine called Los Cuatro Vientos, renowned for its cecina, handmade tortillas, and café de la olla," he replied, almost licking his lips at the thought of the culinary delight about to take place. Aline knew that *cecina* was a type of regionally prepared meat. *Qué rico,* she thought. Her mouth started watering, too.

"Sounds great."

The place was packed with a myriad of diverse patrons: federal police officers, truck drivers, families, some unsavory-looking characters outfitted à la drug-lord style who were eyeing the law enforcement table, and security personnel from a mining company or two. Aline would later find out that the place was actually a hot spot for narcos stopping for a bite after working up an appetite from kidnapping, executing, or extorting something from people. The food was delicious, and in a short time, they were back on the road.

Nearing the city of Iguala, Aline noticed that the driver was more alert to their surroundings than before.

"Anything unusual about this area?" she asked.

He paused before he spoke. "Lots of narcos and violent confrontations between rival organized crime groups."

Forty-five minutes later, turning right onto a very short dirt road, they entered the town of Mezcala located at the base of the mountain where the mine was situated. Aline felt as if they had crossed an invisible barrier separating one reality from the next. There was a palpable tension in the air. It seemed almost hostile. *Bad karma,* thought Aline.

The population was close to four thousand. Anyone not from the town, let alone foreigners, were considered strangers and looked at with extreme wariness. With the blazing tropical sun above, lots of dogs and livestock loitered aimlessly in the streets in no particular hurry. Unpainted speed bumps seemed to spring up without warning. Young teenagers—even tweens—who were stationed at strategic viewpoints eyed the vehicle.

"Halcones," said the driver. "Hawks. On the payroll of the narcos as lookouts to inform them of any strangers entering their domain."

"Or potential rivals," Aline mumbled.

The road up to the mine was treacherous to say the least—narrow curves, cliffs and chasms, hefty animals sporadically impeding transit, and a blatant lack of guardrails, leaving essentially nothing to stop vehicles from taking one-way dives into the expanse some one hundred fifty meters below. Aline took note of local pickups and vehicles with notably limited braking systems and absent taillights, along with trucks hauling water, cyanide, and other materials up and down from the mine. Of course, there was no evidence of any type of lighting for nighttime travel.

About fifteen minutes up, they came upon the employee campsite on the right. Noticeably armed security personnel with 7.62mm assault rifles stood at the entrance with the air of law enforcement. They were Auxiliary Police from Guerrero commissioned to protect the property of the mine. Twenty minutes further up, they finally reached the main gate to the mine. More armed personnel. As they pulled to a stop, Aline was greeted by the superintendent of site security, a retired colonel from the armed forces with strong ties to the military base in Chilpancingo, approximately fifty kilometers from Mezcala in the direction of Acapulco.

"Buenos días. Mucho gusto," declared the coronel, as he was referred to and addressed by persons on-site, extending his hand.

"Mucho gusto. Aline Belanger, a sus *órdenes*."[8]

"The general manager of the mine is expecting you. Please accompany me to the administration office." As they walked toward the building, Aline observed that the majority of pickups and vehicles—white in color—were covered in distinctive red and brown splashes of earth. Looking down, she noticed a film of red dust already starting to form on her boots. The mine was about twelve hundred meters above sea level, actually situated between the towns of Mezcala and Carrizalillo, surrounded by almost tropical foliage, flora and fauna, and heat and humidity. One underground and two open-pit mines were in continuous operation, producing more than two hundred and fifty thousand ounces of gold per annum.

The MGM, who would later become one of Aline's ever-changing direct-report bosses as VP of the region, was a tall man with broad shoulders in his late forties. He expressed himself with a hint of an accent from the northern state of Durango where he was born. Authoritative in carriage, he quickly sized her up from head to toe.

....

8 *A sus órdenes*—The Spanish equivalent of "at your service."

"So, you're the new regional director of security for the Company?" he asked, extending his hand.

"That's right. Aline Belanger," she answered, looking him squarely in the eye, squeezing his hand harder than she was accustomed to doing.

"Nice grip."

"Thanks. It helps to work out a bit," she said with a smile.

"Mr. Bozeman, our boss, speaks very highly of you and no doubt will expect much from you," he said, almost as if challenging her.

"That's what I'm here for," she replied, resolute in her posture. *Well, it's clear that he's the boss of the mine and wants to make sure that everyone knows it,* she analyzed internally. *No backing down from this guy. Hard facts, rational arguments, and taking immediate control of any situation will be the most appropriate strategy in dealing with him.*

They briefly discussed the intricacies of the site and the problematic nature of the security situation suffered around the mine and in Guerrero in general, which was evident in his concerned, almost anxious facial expression.

"Here's my cell phone number," Aline said confidently. "It's twenty-four seven. Call whenever you need to."

After the meeting, Aline hooked up with the coronel so that he could give her a behind-the-scenes security tour of the installations. Hopping into the passenger seat of the 4x4 pickup, she instinctively fastened her seat belt.

"It's good that you are aware of vehicle safety," said the coronel as he buckled himself in. The Golden Rule in all of our mines."

He hit the horn consecutively three times, the standard when putting any vehicle on-site into reverse. The pickup slowly backed up and then incorporated into the left lane of the two-directional roadway, making its way toward the underground mine.

"All vehicles must drive on the left side of any throughway in order for the haul truck drivers to be able to see you and not steamroll over your vehicle when they are taking curves." Sure enough, as they took the first curve in the road, a Caterpillar haul truck was making its way toward them. The motorized beast was massive, towering at six and a half meters with a nominal payload capacity of two hundred forty tons and an overall length of 12.9 meters. It dwarfed the pickup. It reminded Aline of a big Tonka truck from her childhood, only this one was real. *Good idea to stay to the left,* she thought.

****

October. Back in Zacatecas. Negotiations with the leaders of the *ejidos* were on shaky ground in terms of payment for land use.[9] Local and national media coverage of the enduring discord depicted the Company as pirates of the twenty-first century, profiting from the innocent communities, which was clearly not the case. At the forefront of the negotiations—and

9 *Ejidos*—Land held in common by the local community.

eventual lawsuits—were advisors and legal counsel of dubious origins with proven ulterior motives. The problem would become so convoluted and severe that at one point it almost forced the permanent closure of the mine.

Mixed into the disarray was a persistent fear of information being leaked or conversations being illegally monitored by the opposing camp. On one occasion, Aline received a request to contact a TSCM service provider in order to carry out an electronic sweep of the MGM's quarters and a number of boardrooms, as there were rumors that conversations were being overheard.[10] She knew at once whom she was going to call.

"Hello, my friend. It's Aline."

"Hola, amiga," said the president & CEO of a U.S.-based company that provided specialized security consulting and services. "How's Mexico treating you?"

"Just fine. How are things in the North? Still working out of Milton?"

"Nope. I'm in Cleveland, Ohio now."

"Great."

"I heard you were working for the Company, protecting their gold and stuff."

"Yup. Plenty to keep safe," she said.

"Ha, that's an understatement," he laughed. "I'm sure that you're knee deep in it all the time."

"Try neck deep. But anyway, you know how it is with security folk. Better to keep them busy so they stay out of trouble," she joked.

....

10 TSCM—Technical Surveillance Counter-Measures, which is the process utilized to detect the presence of technical surveillance devices.

"That's for sure. So what can I do for you?" he asked.

"I know it's really short notice, but I'm going to need a sweep done at one of our facilities located in the Zacatecas desert. Just an in-and-out job, and the cover will be general services involving maintenance to the air systems."

"Sounds pretty straightforward. Who's going to know about it?"

"Only the regional SVP, the mine general manager, and myself. Not even site security will be involved. I want to keep it as low profile as possible."

"Got it."

Within a week, a specialist was flown in.

Possible espionage aside, Aline was privy to a chat between some colleagues from the Company's Community Relations Department while she grabbed a coffee in a small kitchenette located in the admin building of the Zacatecas mine. One of them was relating how a discussion had gone with a local community member who lived nearby.

"So I said to the guy, 'Yes, but the Company has provided the community with cemented roadways, electricity, social and educational programs, running water, and indoor plumbing,' and you know what he told me?" he asked disbelievingly.

"No, what?"

"He scoffed and said, 'Why would I want to have a toilet in my house? I eat in my house.'"

"Really? That's just crazy."

Actually, it's not, Aline thought. The Company's approach was simply not taking into account the perspective of the communities around their operations, a practice they would disengage from again and again.

Aline finished her coffee and threw the empty cup into one of the neatly arranged recycling bins. As she was not able to make rounds of the installations on her last visit to the mine due to the blockade, she was eager to do so, particularly to see where *doré* bars were produced.[11] It took about ten minutes to arrive at a grey and rudimentary-looking building somewhat isolated from the other mine operations. Stepping out of the vehicle, she noticed that the structure was enclosed by a steel mesh fence that stood 2.4 meters in height with coiled barbed wire on top and a security camera mounted on one of the posts.

"So, this is where the bars are made?" Aline asked.

"Yes. This is the mine's refinery," said the head of security. He pressed the button installed on the gatepost, and they were buzzed in.

A short walk up to the steel-plated door. Another button. The sound of someone unlocking the heavy mechanism. The reinforced door opened slowly, and they were met by the guard on duty.

"Buenos días," greeted the guard.

"Buenos días," said Aline as they entered the small, secured area. Once inside, the guard registered their names in the logbook and led them through another locked door to the vault, open and empty. She quickly observed two ugly and dull-looking grey bars on the floor. They seemed very heavy.

11 *Doré*—A semi-pure alloy of gold and silver in cast bars weighing approximately eighty to one hundred kilograms depending on the mine.

"What are those?" she asked.

"Doré bars," answered the security head.

"And what are they worth?" Aline breathed deeply, trying not to blow a gasket as she waited for the answer.

"Oh, about 1.3 million U.S. dollars," he said almost proudly.

"Hmm." *No-brainer question coming up here,* thought Aline. "So shouldn't the bars be in the vault, not lying on the floor?" she asked, feeling irritated.

"Yes, but the vault lock is not working."

Aline rolled her eyes and turned to the guard on duty. "And how long has the doré been lying around?"

"Oh, about two to three days."

"Wow." *Mental note*: *If the site security guys didn't have a problem with leaving the most valuable product of the mine out in the open, then that in and of itself is a serious problem.*

Returning to the security office, still a bit astounded by what she had just witnessed, Aline decided to head for the canteen. It was time for lunch.

Her cell phone vibrated with an incoming call. The screen flashed.

MGM—Guerrero Mine

"Go ahead," said Aline, standing up from the table to separate herself from the noisy clatter.

"We have a kidnapping situation. Two of our employees. What should we do?"

"If you haven't already done so, please contact the regional SVP to brief him on the incident." She didn't want him to get blindsided by a call from the head office inquiring about an incident that he might not yet be aware of. "And please, only provide him with information that has been confirmed. In the meantime, I will notify the director of Corporate Security and gather more information from the superintendent of security on-site."

Within a few minutes, Aline had put together the most accurate data that she could, jotting down only hard facts, making sure to avoid opinions, suppositions, and hearsay. Opening the contact list in her cell phone, she started to go through the registries. She stopped at a number from the U.K. and—as per protocol—dialed the London Desk of the retained K&R service, which was short for "kidnap and ransom."

"Hello. This is Aline Belanger, Regional Director of Security for the Company. Am I speaking to the duty officer?"

"Yes. How may I be of assistance, ma'am?"

"I was informed approximately ten minutes ago of the possible kidnapping of two employees from our mine in Guerrero. They were apparently at a local party last night in Mezcala, and around 12:45 a.m. this morning, they were supposedly abducted at gunpoint by a small group of men."

"Has there been a ransom demand made yet?" he asked.

"As far as we know at this moment, the Company has not been contacted by the kidnappers. They only contacted the family members of the two employees, and they are apparently asking for two million pesos."

"Okay. Do you have any indication or substantiated information that would indicate that this is directed toward, or has anything to do with, the Company?"

"No. It seems to be focused specifically on these two employees, particularly because one of them is related to the mayor of the town."

"Okay. I have a member of our team standing by who will be dispatched to Mexico as soon as we have the go-ahead from Mr. Straddler."

"Understood."

In the end, there was a stand-down on the intervention from the U.K. The family members of the two persons put together a MXN $1.2 million ransom and paid the kidnappers, at which point the victims were released.

****

A week later, Aline was on a short visit to the Guerrero mine. Mr. Bozeman had requested that she conduct a sit-down meeting with the managerial team. She could see and feel lots of anxiety concerning the security situation around the mine and the well-being of the employees, including the managers themselves.

"Let me assure you that we are doing our very best to improve security for everyone here at the mine," she said. She tried to pacify the somewhat antagonistic crowd by sharing with them the regional security initiatives that she had going in the short and medium term, which regrettably was met with hostility and contempt.

"And you think that's going to make a difference?" asked the manager of finance, looking at her belligerently.

"Come on," added the head of the refinery. "The Company wants us to work here, so it should make it safe for us, no?"

The group in general took a hard-line stance in demanding a solution to a problem endemic to the state and to Mexico itself, which would become a prevalent posture at the mine. They insisted that it was the responsibility of the Security Department to ensure that they would be safe and secure in the current dangerous environment.

Understandable, yet ill-conceived, mused Aline. *How can a company guarantee the security of employees outside of the mine? That would be the equivalent of promising someone that nothing would happen to them when they stepped out of their home every morning in a neighborhood known for criminal activity.* She would continually have to remind employees and management alike that the mines were located in conflictive areas, and the associated inherent risk would have to be accepted. Period.

"Well, that went rather poorly," said Aline to the coronel as they walked down the steps from the meeting room.

"*Sí*. They are scared and unfortunately are trying to find someone that will make the threat go away, and you being the Company's newly hired regional security director, they now see you as that person."

"Wonderful."

"How about a café?" he asked, trying to make her feel a little better. "I know a place in Mezcala."

"Sounds nice."

They drove down to the town, and the coronel parked the pickup in front of a locale on a small street. The place was empty except for the owner, a pleasant-looking older woman with keen little eyes tucked away behind round cheeks, humming and cleaning the counter with a towel.

"Buenas tardes, Coronel," she said with familiarity.

"Buenas tardes, señora."

"And who is this lovely young lady with you?" she asked with a smile.

"This is my colleague, Aline," he said, intentionally not introducing her as his superior.

"Mucho gusto," said Aline.

"What can I get you?"

"Dos cafés, por favor," replied the coronel.

"Claro que sí. Coming right up."

They sat down at a table in the corner, and shortly thereafter, the aroma of freshly made coffee permeated the air.

"Coronel," said a voice on the portable radio hanging on his utility belt.

"Adelante para Coronel," he responded.

"We need your signed authorization for a supplier trying to leave the mine with some material."

"On my way. I'll be back in a while. Shouldn't take too long."

"Okay," said Aline.

As the coronel stepped out, the owner brought the coffees to the table.

"Hmm. I'm sure he won't return before his coffee gets cold. Would you mind if I join you?" the owner asked.

"Not at all. Por favor."

The *señora* sat down and opened a few sugar packets, which she carefully poured into her mug. "So, how long have you been with the Company?"

"Oh, just a short while. I'm still new."

"Well, I'm sure you will like it. Just be careful. There are a lot of hombres malos here around the mine that like to cause problems."

"Really?" queried Aline, deliberately leaning forward to demonstrate that her interest was piqued.

"Yes," said the owner, happy for a reason to gossip. "You know, this region has always had, well...narcos because of the drogas. They come and go, always fighting for territory."

"Wow, that's pretty unfortunate, and I'm sure that each group has its own way of doing business," said Aline.

"Sí," confirmed the woman, sipping her coffee. "For example, the one that is now pushing for control is run by a man called El Líder. We don't see him here very often because they say that he lives in Acapulco, but he does have a local guy. Teniente."

Aline focused her attention even more. "And what's he like?" she asked casually.

"Handsome enough. He likes the ladies and flashy things, like gold and expensive cars. They say he has lots of bars and some hotels and working girls." The woman paused, staring for a few seconds as if trying to remember something. "Yes," she continued. "One of the bars is quite nearby in Chilpancingo. I think it's called La Katrina."

"Ah," said Aline, somewhat disinterestedly. She shifted the topic. "So, were you born here in Mezcala?"

"Oh yes. My whole family. My brothers and sisters and our parents and their parents."

"It must be difficult and scary to have these problems here."

"Yes it is, but we manage. This is our home, and we are not going anywhere."

****

In a few days it would be Halloween. The mining convention in Acapulco was in full swing. Approximately four hundred employees and their spouses were herded from one venue to the next. A couple of weeks prior to the event, Aline had issued an internal bilingual communication of do's and do not's, including a list of contacts in case of emergency.

"Yeah, you know foreigners when traveling to tropical destinations," said Mr. Straddler, calling from his home office in Lethbridge, Alberta. "Always getting lost or doing something stupid that they shouldn't be doing, then complaining that no one had told them they couldn't do so in the first place."

"Yeah, that pretty much sums it up," said Aline.

Upon her arrival forty-eight hours before the commencement of the convention, she re-established contacts made on the previous visit, carried out "route recces," or reconnaissance, with the security drivers, confirmed shuttles, and administered employee event badges. And of course, no convention—at least not one in Mexico—could go without the standard group of *edecanes*, or "hostesses." These were attractive young ladies attired in body-tight, red and white dresses and heels hired by the Company to greet employees and provide them with information. Not surprisingly, during the course of the event, it was rumored that a couple of the girls were willing and able to provide private entertainment at a reasonable price.

As chance would have it, even though Aline's internal communication clearly stated not to wander far from the hotel or frequent establishments of a questionable nature, on the first night, a young lady from the regional office—Lara from the HR Department to be precise—was unaccounted for and was not answering her cell phone.

"That's right," said Aline, reconfirming information for the hotel security manager. "The last she was seen or heard from was about three hours ago."

"Okay. We'll give it a bit more time, and then we'll enter her room to see if we might find something that would give us a sign as to her whereabouts, of course in the presence of yourself or someone from your team."

"Thank you. That's very courteous of you," said Aline, now turning to Karmyn. "And you said that you've been trying to call her on her cell phone, correct?"

"Yes. I wanted her to help me with something, but there was no answer."

"Did it ring, or did it go straight to voicemail?"

"No. There was a normal ring."

"Why don't we try her room again? Maybe she fell asleep."

As they called from the front desk without success and planned their next steps, Lara walked into the hotel lobby. "What's going on, guys?" she asked innocently.

"Looking for you," replied Aline, annoyed. "Remember the published security recommendations where we requested that people inform us where they are going if it's somewhere other than the event or hotel?"

"Oh yeah," she answered guiltily. She had apparently been shopping and lost track of time. She had also forgotten her cell phone in her room.

Aline turned around, shook her head, and crossed the enormous lobby to a little coffee shop and bistro. "That deserves an iced mocha," she said to herself.

"Hola," Aline said, passing one of the hostesses who looked bored out of her mind.

"Hola, buenas noches," replied the girl.

Enjoying her cold beverage, Aline recalled something that Mr. Straddler had mentioned in their last conversation about the convention. "And just FYI, you will have an employee at the venue named Bob. Good fellow. Unfortunately, he seems to have a streak of bad luck that follows him around wherever he goes."

"How so?" she had asked.

"Well, at the last convention a couple of years ago, some venomous spider or insect bit him, and he had to be rushed to the emergency room. Then, at another event, he suffered a severe case of food poisoning."

"Bad mojo, I guess. I'll keep an eye out for him."

Two days after the Lara incident, Aline was startled from her sleep by a call on her cell phone.

"Hello?" she said sleepily.

"Aline?" said Karmyn. "We have a situation with one of our employees, Bob. Apparently, he's having sharp pains in his abdomen. He's being looked at right now by the hotel physician."

"Okay. On my way." Aline put on a pair of shorts and a T-shirt and headed for the medical center.

"What do you think, Doc?" she asked when she arrived.

"Puede ser apendicitis," he said.

"Should we move him to a hospital?"

"Um...my personal recommendation would be to send him to a medical facility in Mexico City. The hospitals here are not the most reliable and less so during the weekend. The patient is stable, but I would say that he should be moved tonight."

"Muchas gracias, Doctor."

Aline arranged for one of the security drivers to take Bob to the airport and help him get checked in while she coordinated an ambulance to be on standby at the airport in Mexico City, with paramedics waiting to receive and transport him to the hospital.

The next morning, Bob was admitted into surgery for an appendectomy.

That evening, there was a formal dinner and concert on the convention's agenda. The performing artist was Yuri, a famous and very charismatic Mexican singer, actress, and TV host. Mr. Bozeman and his pleasant wife of Mongolian descent were in line waiting to enter the venue, making small talk with the MGM from Guerrero and his wife.

As the line advanced, Mr. Bozeman searched his jacket pockets for his tickets. Looking nervously at his wife, Aline overheard him say, "Are you sure you don't have the tickets with you?"

"No," she said. "The last time I saw them they were on the table in the hotel room." Aline knew that it would take at least forty-five minutes to get to the hotel and back, so she called Karmyn, who was already inside the venue, on her cell to ask for two additional tickets. Meanwhile, her boss, looking around in desperation, was turning different shades of red and about to spew out some inevitable profanity when Aline spotted Karmyn coming out from a side door, tickets in hand.

"Gracias, chica."

"De nada."

Aline turned around, walked back into the line, and passed the tickets from behind to an astonished SVP. "Here you go, sir," she said calmly, resolving the issue quickly and quietly.

****

Aline was en route to the Golden Triangle—*el Triangulo Dorado*—the gold-bearing region situated between the states of Chihuahua, Sinaloa, and Durango, which she knew was infamous for the established presence of organized crime, violence, and lawlessness.[12]

In a Best Western in Los Mochis, Sinaloa, Aline was chatting quietly over dinner with Clark, the new regional security manager whom she had recently hired for the northern states. A trusted former employee from the automotive industry and expert in hapkido, he was taking on the role of immediate superior for the security guys working at the Chihuahua and Zacatecas mines, in addition to providing support to the local offices in the region.

"So, how does it feel working in the mining industry?" she asked.

"Awesome," he replied enthusiastically. "More so because I have another chance to be a part of your

12 There was no legitimate law enforcement in this area, and the nearest military base was located in Parral, Chihuahua, about seven hours and forty-five minutes away by road.

team." He had known Aline—or really, he knew of her—even before meeting her in person.

At her last MMA career fight in the city of Puebla against the national judo champion, Clark had seats almost ringside. The bout was set according to old-school rules: mixed weight class and one round lasting thirty minutes that could only be stopped by submission, knockout, or technical knockout, with no eye-gouging or biting. Everything else was pretty much kosher.[13] The crowd, characteristically xenophobic, was already loud and disorderly. Aline's trainer, a long-retired golden gloves boxing champion, adjusted her hand wraps and placed the open-fingered gloves onto her hands. Aline had spent the last three months training with him at his boxing gym from 4:00 a.m. to 6:00 a.m. and then again in the late afternoon, improving her handwork, speed, and overall physical conditioning.

As the second-to-last fight of the night ended by submission, Aline shifted her weight from one foot to another, anticipating the announcement of the main event and her cue to enter. She was slightly optimistic that there wouldn't be too much build-up of the fact that she was Canadian, but this notion was quickly quashed by the announcer.

"Directly from Canada, here to fight our national champion, Aline Belanger!"

....

13 Submission—A fighter trapped in a submission hold can tap out on his or her opponent's body or mat; KO—A fighter loses consciousness from an opponent's strikes; TKO—A fight is ended by the referee when a fighter is no longer defending himself or herself.

She encountered raucous boos and heckling as she made her way to the ring, on occasion having to physically move people who obstructed her path. As she entered the quadrilateral—octagonal cages were still not the norm here—she sized up her opponent: Big. Not quite in need of an anti-doping test as had happened in previous fights, but taller and heavier than Aline by about seven inches and ten to twelve kilograms. Looking up, she saw herself on the big screen, and then focused on what was about to go down. With alternating feet, she pounded the canvas, as was customary for her, while she waited for the bell.

Mat feels a bit unstable, she thought. *Oh well.*

Ding! Pouncing forward, Aline advanced to the center of the ring, quickly closing the distance and wrapping her forearms around her opponent's neck in a Thai-boxing clinch. Dropping her weight downward, she threw her adversary to the mat. Attempting to swiftly apply a rear-naked chokehold, she inopportunely switched her arm position, trying to lock in the strangulation, giving her opponent just enough time to secure Aline's right leg. Bolting upward, her adversary lifted Aline up into the air, and with the same momentum, came crashing down backward on top of her, weight, and all.[14]

Hijo de la chingada, she thought.

Momentarily dazed, Aline took five to six hits to the head as her opponent ascended to the mount position.

....

14 Rear-naked chokehold—A submission hold used in mixed martial arts that, if applied correctly, will force the opponent to submit, or pass out, in a matter of seconds.

While covering herself, Aline managed to dislodge her opponent and get back up. On her feet, she regained her composure and launched two quick kicks using her right shin to her opponent's left-outside thigh, causing pain and temporary motor dysfunction, and followed up with a succession of effective hooks to the side of the head that sent her foe sprawling to the canvas. Gaining the mount position, Aline unleashed a barrage of punishing punches to the head, with no visible defense from her opponent, whose body was halfway out of the ring. The referee quickly intervened, tackling Aline into the ropes and stopping the bout as a TKO at the forty-seven-second mark.

Standing, arm raised in victory by the referee, Aline descended from the ring. Still hyped from her adrenaline gushing, she surged toward the locker room, this time with no impeding bodies, as the crowd miraculously opened a pathway for her.

****

The hotel where Aline and Clark were lodged was small and clean, with a surprising number of miners or persons having dealings with the mining industry. In the morning, they would take a shuttle to El Fuerte, Sinaloa, about an hour-and-a-half drive, and from there, take a Company plane to the mine.

The open-pit mine, the remotest of the Company's operations, was nestled in the southwest mountain range of Chihuahua near the locality of Tubares in the municipality of Urique. The pilot of the DHC-6 Twin Otter was an elderly man, tall and slim, with a moustache, cowboy hat, boots, and a pronounced northern regional accent.[15] Aline saw forested mountains in every direction, occasionally interrupted by clandestine airstrips and harvested fields of illicit cannabis or opium poppy. As the Twin Otter descended, Aline tried to identify the mine from above to no avail, although within minutes the open pit became discernible in the arboraceous landscape. The aircraft circled and aligned itself with the so-called landing strip—more precisely, a sliver of narrow terrain—about seven hundred meters in length, which ended abruptly in a cliff wall.

Walking toward the security gate, Aline smiled and nodded hello to some of the employees waiting anxiously in line to board the aircraft after completing their 10x4 or 14x7 work tours.[16] Security personnel carrying 7.62mm assault rifles in khaki uniforms and baseball caps to match were distributed throughout the airfield. By the time the new arrivals had checked in with security and loaded their gear onto the transport, the Twin was already picking up speed and heading down the runway, departing for civilization. *Welcome to the real boonies*, she thought.

Aline opted to travel with the security supervisor in his assigned pickup instead of taking the transport. This was also her first opportunity to chat with a member of her team.

....

15 The Twin Otter—A Canadian-made, nineteen-passenger capacity, STOL (Short Takeoff and Landing) utility aircraft, often used for mines located in remote mountainous areas.

16 Because of the location of the mine, work tours were scheduled as ten days on/four days off or fourteen days on/seven days off, respectively.

"What are the other ways that can be used to get to and from the mine?" she queried.

"Not too many. You can take a flight from Hermosillo in the state of Sonora or the city of Chihuahua."

"How about road travel?"

The supervisor paused for a minute. "Very dangerous because of the narcos. You wouldn't want to be running into them. If there was no other way and you were here in the mine and you had, for example, a medical emergency, you could drive to Choix, Sinaloa in the southwest about six and a half hours away or to Chihuahua City in the northeast, which would take about seven hours and forty-five minutes."

"Got it." *Translation: Avoid road travel whenever possible,* she thought.

It was pretty obvious that the area was isolated. Looking down at her cell phone, Aline saw no bars and a discouraging *sin servicio* message on the screen.

"No cell phone coverage here," said the security supervisor.

"Ni modo," she commented.

According to the supervisor, the local inhabitants were dispersed, fragmented groups of families living in makeshift houses spread out over an enormous vastness.

"We had some problems a while back with a crime group trying to gain presence in the area, but it was taken care of," he said.

"How's that?" she asked.

"Well, rumor has it that information filtered out from within the mine that this new group was making demands on the Company. In doing so, they infringed on the established cartel. Payback was swiftly executed as the newcomers were sought out and literally eliminated." Aline later deduced that the source of the information leak was most likely the female cousin of the drug lord who was working in the Administration Department.

Aline didn't say anything for a few minutes, trying to assimilate what she had just heard while the engine of the pickup hummed along uninterruptedly in its ascent up the mountain. As if this recent piece of news was no more than a weather update, the supervisor continued with his tour guide remarks.

"The region is also home to the indigenous Tarahumara population, a quiet and unassuming people, usually keeping to themselves. They are renowned for their prowess in running great distances."

"Ah yes, the Rarámuri, of course."[17] They were ultra-runners with remarkable speed and conditioning that ran unprecedented distances—eighty to one hundred sixty kilometers on any given day—in rudimentary, handmade, sandal-like footwear called *huaraches*.

As they reached the uppermost point of the mine property, Aline spotted a security guard on his cell phone stationed at a lookout post, somewhat masked by the surrounding foliage.

"I thought that there was no cell phone coverage here."

"Surprisingly, only at this exact location do signals come in and out sporadically," said the supervisor. She thought to herself that this would probably be the most

17 *Rarámuri*–Loosely translated, it means "runners on foot" or "those who run fast" from Uto-Aztecan, which is a Native American language found in Mexico and the western United States.

eagerly sought-after location posting of the security personnel. As she got out of the pickup, she walked cautiously toward the edge of a nearby precipice. Quiet. Serene. No movement. Nothing. It made sense to grow marijuana and opium poppy here.

By the time they finished surveying the area, the sun had started to descend slowly below the tree line of the mountains, a good sign that dinner was probably somewhere around the corner.

The employee canteen was rather small, and many of the tables were already filled with miners, most of them scarfing down their meals while hypnotically staring at the television screens mounted in the corners of the room. The Bandamax channel blared *banda* music videos that portrayed sultry Latinas with pouting mouths and well-endowed figures outfitted in attire that seemed to have accidentally gone through the dryer. *This explains the dazed expressions of the viewers,* she thought.

The food was good and had a home-cooked touch, tortillas and all. Exiting the dining area, the supervisor unloaded Aline's gear from the pickup, and they walked up toward the employee housing—small, connected, one-room, bungalow-type structures, each with its own bathroom. Aline was surprised that the door was unlocked.

"Is there a key for the room?"

"No. No keys for any of them. It's pretty safe here."

There was a brief moment of silence, unintentionally creating dramatic effect as a heavily armed security guard walked by. *That's reassuring*, Aline thought sarcastically. *Security personnel patrolling with firepower that could easily penetrate the row of feeble rooms from an accidental discharge, perhaps provoked by a stumble in the low lighting of the campground.*

"Good night. Sleep well."

"Yeah, you too."

The room was warm and humid, and Aline noticed that the ceiling had several openings between its panels just big enough to let in marauding members of the arachnid family, which were widespread in the region. And it just happened to be tarantula season. "Great. Nothing like having a furry spider fall on your head while you sleep," she mulled. As any good security officer, and/or person slightly out of their element, Aline took out her portable tactical flashlight and meticulously scanned the area under the bed. After the zone was cleared, she put the first rule of potential cohabitation with fauna into effect by ruffling the pillow and bedsheets vigorously to reduce the chances of any unwanted guest having taken up lodgings for the night. Everything okay. Second rule: Make sure that your boots are turned upside down, and elevate them if possible. *Sound advice.*

Dawn came early, and Aline got out of bed sleepily. To avoid walking around the room barefoot, she slipped into her sandals and went to the bathroom. The availability of hot water in the shower was unexpectedly quick and very welcome. After getting dressed and packing her gear, she opened the door to the room and stepped out into a thick wall of fog.

Unexpected.

Walking down to the canteen for breakfast, she ran into the supervisor's 2 I/C.

"Morning. How was your night?" he asked.

"Fine, thanks. Do you think the plane will be on schedule?"

"Hmm. Depends on whether the fog will lift before the cut-off time for flights entering or leaving the mine," he replied.

Awesome.

Other than the fog, which Aline later learned was quite common for the area, flights were prohibited after 1:00 p.m. since wind conditions were too strong to safely maneuver the planes.

The fog did eventually lift, and Aline made her way to the airfield contently. While waiting for the Twin to arrive, she took out her cell phone and snapped a photo of a billboard that showed an absurdly simplistic map depicting the general location of the mine. *All that's missing is the "You Are Here" symbol found in shopping mall screen directories,* she observed.

As the security officer finished going through Aline's knapsack, she entered the small guardhouse and stepped onto the scale where another officer jotted down her weight.

"Hopefully that extra helping of tortillas at breakfast won't make that much of a difference," she said to the guard, who laughed hesitantly, not knowing whether she was joking or not. The weigh-in was SOP, or standard operating procedure, to ensure that weight limits were being respected for the aircraft. Stepping down, Aline walked to the cordoned-off line and took her place among the other employees.

A few minutes later, they heard the faint din of the Twin approaching the mine. The plane came to a complete stop, and the copilot proceeded to open the door. Passengers started to disembark. As they walked to the security checkpoint, some smiled and nodded. Others didn't. Aline passed her baggage to the copilot, who was arranging space in the cargo hold, and headed to the steps of the Twin.

"Buenos días, Capi," she said to the captain of the aircraft.

"Buenos días, Señorita Aline. Nice to see you again."

CHAPTER 3

Six months into the job, Aline was getting a pretty good handle on things. She had just gotten back from a corporate security meeting in Phoenix, Arizona hosted by a major mining company. The purpose of the event was to gather a cluster of security representatives from various mining corporations to discuss the challenges of working in different regions. Putting the final toiletries into her bag for her next outing, she smiled as she recalled sitting in the pleasantly air-conditioned boardroom of the corporate skyscraper and the reaction of the group when one of them asked, "So, where do you operate in Mexico?"

"Guerrero, Chihuahua, and Zacatecas," she rattled off mechanically.

"Oh," said a number of them, inadvertently twisting their mouths in discomfort.

"That must keep you awake at night," added another.

"You could say that," she replied. "Organized crime, NGOs, local communities demanding increases in royalties, the nuances of acquiring subsoil permits, on-top special taxation (equivalent to eight percent for extraction industries), disgruntled unions, local auto-defense groups—you know, armed vigilantes—and narcos requesting the mine hire family members as a sign of good faith, whatever that means, just to name a few."

"Sure hope they're paying you enough," said the chair of the meeting, grinning.

****

Aline zipped the bag up and headed out the door to the waiting Company driver who would take her to the Guerrero mine where she would be conducting an interrogation as part of an internal investigation concerning diesel fraud.

"Pinche calor," said the coronel as they sat in the security trailer located close to the entrance of the underground mine. The portable air-conditioning unit was buzzing away but had little effect on the sweltering 38°C humid heat.

"Sí," Aline replied, wiping a trickle of sweat that ran down the side of her face.

The coronel continued. "You know, as it is viernes social, a few of us have planned to drive to Chilpancingo in the afternoon for a late lunch, then go out for a few drinks and stay the night. It would be an honor if you would join us."

"Absolutely. Sounds like fun."

The *tacos de canasta* and cold beers really hit the spot.

"Salud," they said, raising their bottles and extending them toward Aline.

"Salud." Leaning over to the coronel, she then asked in a lowered tone, "So, tell me. How extensive is the problem of organized crime here in Guerrero?"

"Híjole," he said, motioning with his right hand in a quick, back-and-forth movement, signifying the severity of the problem. "Muy, pero muy grande. The region is historically known for the harvesting of amapola extracted from the poppy flower."[18]

"I've heard the word before but don't understand it very well," she replied.

"Let me explain. Amapola flourishes pretty much all year round. When the flowers are still unripe, they have these capsules that are cut or scored with a very thin knife, and raw opium gum oozes out through the cuts. The gum is then scraped from the plant, dried, and later processed into opium, or heroin. Once the flower itself dries, the seeds are collected and used for the sowing period."

"Interesting. And what kind of impact has this had on the Company?"

"Well, there's the ever-present crime gangs trying to control los campos in the area, provoking violent exchanges with rivals or the police and military. Last week, for example, the ID of an employee was found in a poppy field nearby. It is quite common for employees to take vacation time or sick leave from the mine to harvest the gum, which pays very well, and these absences unfortunately affect Company production."

"I'm sure. Hey," started Aline, trying to lighten up the discussion a little, "someone at the mine told me that there's an enjoyable bar here in the city. I can't

....

18 The state of Guerrero is considered the country's number-one producer of poppy gum—*goma de opio*—with yearly production estimated at MXN $1.2 billion.

remember exactly what it was called. Some kind of girl's name. I think it starts with the letter K. Kara, Katia..."

"Ah. You mean La Katrina."

"Yes, that was it!" she exclaimed.

"*Sí*. I know it, and it's just down the road from here."

As the sun set, Aline and the coronel made their way to the bar. Live music was playing, and the place was already filled with patrons who had started the weekend early. Aline observed a small group of local girls in high heels and miniskirts working the bar, looking for potential clients. As Aline was ushered to a table, she noticed a tall guy smoking Marlboros sitting with an attractive *morena* with dyed-blonde hair in a corner booth. He was wearing a thick gold chain and rings, short-cropped hair, and a well-kept handlebar moustache. She was aware that he was looking at her, and once their glances crossed, she didn't look down but calmly kept her gaze fixed. As she and the coronel ordered their drinks, she observed two brutish-looking fellows sitting at the bar with their backs to her, making eye contact in the mirrored wall with the guy who had been observing her.

A couple of hours—and rounds—later, Aline got up and went to the ladies' room. Dark. Leaving the stall, she was startled when two males entered the bathroom and locked the door behind them. She quickly recognized the two as the guys who had been sitting at the bar.

"Te ves muy guapa, güerita," said one of them as he stepped closer to her. Instead of backing away, which would have been a natural defensive response, Aline maneuvered forward, lowering her body slightly, almost imperceptibly, before springing up like a cat in a sudden, explosive burst, launching a crushing left hook to the brachial plexus of her surprised assailant, rendering him unconscious before his body hit the floor. The second guy, stunned by the fact that his buddy had been neutralized, didn't have time to avoid the two successive, arcing right elbows that she threw, which came smashing down onto his nose. Her right hand came up instantly, securing his hair from behind. Pivoting her body to the left, she slammed his head downward onto the edge of the ceramic sink, the impact producing an unnatural thump. She released his hair, letting him crumple into a heap next to his *cuate*.

"Putos," she said, looking at herself in the mirror and washing off the droplets of blood that had splattered onto her cheek. She dried her face and unlocked the door.

"You were gone for quite a while," said the coronel. "Everything okay?"

"Just fine. How about we head out?"

"Me parece bien."

They paid the tab and walked toward the exit, Aline feeling the stare on the back of her neck from the guy sitting in the booth.

****

March in Toronto was cold. Bloody cold at -30°C. Aline had been invited by the Prospectors & Developers Association of Canada to originally speak on corruption in Mexico. However, a last-minute confirmation from a few Mexican officials who would be partaking in the convention required a minor adjustment to the title of her presentation—the less controversial "Bribery in Mexico." Thick coat, scarf, mittens, and earmuffs in order, she opened the door of the convention center and stepped into the frigid air with Tim Hortons coffee in hand, as any proper Canadian would. Winter days in the North were very short, and the sun had already begun to set as she hailed a cab on the busy street.

"Where to, Miss?"

"King Street West, please."

Prior to departing from Mexico, the MGM from the Guerrero mine and the VP of operations arranged for a private meeting with the president & CEO of another Canadian mining corporation at their headquarters in downtown Toronto. As both companies were technically neighbors in terms of their operations in Guerrero, they had agreed to meet and discuss common concerns, security measures, and potential collaboration with military and law enforcement. Arriving in the lobby of the building, she coincided with the MGM and VP, both shriveled and red-nosed from the climate.

"Cold enough for ya?" she laughed.

They entered the elevator, and she pressed the button for the seventh floor.

"Hello, Aline," smiled the director of Community Relations as the elevator doors opened.

"Hi, how are you? Nice to finally meet you."

"You too," he said as he led them down the hall to the meeting room. Aline had established contact with the director a couple of months back over phone and e-mail, but this was the first time that they had met in person.

"Please come in," said the director. "Everyone, I'd like you to meet our president & CEO." They took their seats, and fresh doughnuts were brought in. *Well-thought-out and nice complement to the coffee,* Aline mused.

"So, let's talk security," said the president.

****

Returning to the South, several violent clashes between rival crime groups in Guerrero set Aline in motion. She set out toward the affected mine to make sure that risks were being mitigated as best as possible. Six days later, she found herself in Acapulco, attending a prescheduled meeting with the regional coordinator of the Federal Police.

Acapulco had become dicey, more so than usual. Violence, kidnappings, executions, body parts washing up here and there on the coastline, and narco *mantas*—or handwritten banners, hanging up with the usual profanity issuing warnings to rival groups—were all present while the Army, Navy, and Federal Police continually patrolled the once peaceful port city.

The plan was to get in and out of the meeting and fly back to Mexico City ASAP. As the prearranged Company driver and armored vehicle made its way along the main boulevard, Aline could feel the tension in the air. Her co-passengers from the Company were the VP of operations and the MGM from the Guerrero mine. As the driver pulled over, she was astonished that the Regional Federal Police Office was located on the second floor of an open, touristy mall.

The entrance to the office was a regular plate-glass door with no access control devices or CCTV cameras whatsoever. Unusual. They were greeted by a uniformed officer at the reception desk and invited to sit down while the regional coordinator was informed of their arrival.

Aline was puzzled. *Why are they so exposed?* she thought. *Either they have no perception of the present threat level in the city, which would be totally ludicrous, or they feel protected in their environment, perhaps due to ties with criminal entities.* One way or the other, she felt uncomfortable.

After a few minutes, the regional coordinator received them with proper political protocol and entourage in tow.

"Mucho gusto. I am the regional coordinator of the Federal Police for the state of Guerrero. A sus *órdenes*." He was wearing his uniform, complete with shining badge and metal rank bars, impeccably polished black shoes, pressed pants, and a well-maintained, semiautomatic sidearm—a Beretta 92FS. As they went through the usual pleasantries and took their seats around a long table with rounded edges, Aline could not help but notice the Rolex on the coordinator's tanned arm, a bit out of his salary range.

They discussed recent security incidents near the mine and concerns that they had for the safety of the Company's personnel.

As the discussion continued, the coordinator interjected. "Yes, I understand your concerns, but all incidents must be declared officially in writing by means of a registered legal claim to the corresponding public ministry office for any intervention on behalf of the Federal Police." *Oh, nothing more than signing and sealing your own death sentence. Yeah, that's going to happen,* Aline reflected.

After a few more volleys of information, the coordinator called in two additional members from his team: a male and a female who looked like recent high school graduates, even though they were in their early twenties. They were dressed in jeans and T-shirts, and the male had on a baseball cap.

"Let me introduce you to our intelligence officers," said the coordinator. Aline breathed deeply, trying to maintain a neutral expression, although she was quite sure that an uncontrollable eyebrow raise from astonishment had escaped. *So, these are the intelligence officers that will be gathering and processing information from OSINT*[19]*, covert informants, and local contacts while analyzing data, creating taxonomies and profiles of suspected criminals, and identifying and monitoring pertinent social media networks in order to build a solid dossier. Great.*

"All right then," she remarked instead, trying to sound polite. "Are there any additional points of contact that you could provide us with in the event of an incident taking place in real time?"

"Yes. These are my inspectors," he said, motioning to the other officers at the table. "They are available twenty-four seven. Please jot down their names and cell phone numbers." The meeting ended, and Aline was off to the airport to catch the flight back to Mexico City.

****

19 Open Source Intelligence.

6:05 a.m. There was an incoming call on her cell. 733 telephone code, which meant Mezcala, Guerrero.

"Go ahead," said Aline. It was the newly appointed superintendent of security, Joe L., from the Guerrero mine. He was ex-military but not a *coronel.*

"Aline. Two bodies have been found in a vehicle close to the mine. Looks like an execution, and they seem to be employees of the Company."

After issuing a number of standing orders to the superintendent and placing subsequent calls to the SVP and director of Corporate Security, Aline got ready and left for the office. *Good thing it is only three minutes' distance by car or eight minutes by foot if using a shortcut,* she thought.

Aline opened her e-mail session, simultaneously dialing the superintendent at the mine.

"I need you to send me the preliminary report as soon as you have confirmed information."

"Will do," he replied.

Within minutes, Aline was going over the document and the attached graphic photographs. There was no mistaking that it was an execution. The vehicle and the bodies were riddled with bullets. Aside from the perpetrators being really bad shots, it was evident that this was intentional. She slugged back her coffee as she continued to scrutinize the report. She slammed her mug down brusquely and felt a flush of anger and heat cross her neck and face when she came to the last photograph, which clearly showed the new superintendent and one of his officers beside the vehicle, sporting their mine uniforms with the Company logo clear as day. "Bad idea," she said aloud through gritted teeth.

Aline sat there, analyzing the situation rapidly in her mind. Now, explaining that an employee had been unmistakably executed was in and of itself a pretty complicated matter, more so when you have to communicate the incident to the head office in a foreign country where these types of events are almost unheard of. Worse was having to clarify why personnel from your area are in photographs of a crime scene—in Company apparel no less—that has still not been officially investigated by the incumbent authority, which in this case would be the Ministerial Police. She downed the final drops of java and hit redial on the phone.

****

A couple of weeks went by, and Aline was back at the mine in Guerrero, this time with her Canadian boss. The primary reason for the trip was that they had managed to get a meeting with the commanding officer, a brigadier general, of Military Zone 35-A in Chilpancingo. This was significant, as the mine was located within the zone's jurisdiction.

There was the usual wait that went along with military brass receiving a guest. The coronel, who was now functioning as 2 I/C, chatted quietly with Joe L., who was his direct boss, while the Canucks took in the paintings hanging in the corridor.[20]

"Buenas tardes," voiced a high-ranking officer decked out in formal uniform. "The brigadier general will see you now."

20 Canucks—Slang term referring to Canadians.

They entered the office and were presented to the commandant by the coronel, who was actually the contact person organizing the meeting. They all shook hands and sat down in deep leather armchairs around a low, rectangular table. As they were offered beverages, Aline discerned the idiosyncrasies of her environment: a framed photo of the president that hung on the back wall behind a richly engraved wooden desk; a Mexican flag standing at attention in the corner; military swords; methodically arranged photographs on an adjacent wall of the brigadier general with ex-presidents, government officials, and foreign dignitaries; an elegant library lamp on a coffee table; and a score of miniature tanks and army vehicles set neatly in tiny formations along the bookshelves.

Her boss started with the expected formalities, touching on the security problems in the area of the mine, then segued into a promotional plug for the Voluntary Principles on Security and Human Rights.[21]

"At the Guatemala mine, we implemented the Voluntary Principles very successfully and provided corresponding training to the military stationed in the area. It was a mutually beneficial arrangement." They would find out later that this one particular comment was construed as a major insult by the brigadier general, both to himself and the Mexican Army. The coronel later conveyed to the MGM that the commandant had said

21 Designed for the extractive sector, the Voluntary Principles are a set of guidelines applicable to governments, companies, and NGOs that help organizations operate within a framework that encourages respect for human rights.

that Company training imparted to the Guatemalan Army was one thing, but we were in Mexico, and that was something else altogether. Nonetheless, at the time of the meeting, the Canadians had no idea that a blunder had been committed on their part.

The discussion came to an end with the brigadier general agreeing to install a nine-person team in Mezcala to establish military presence in the area. The Company would provide a used pickup truck detailed according to military specs.

As they said their farewells in the parking lot, Aline noticed that the sun had already descended, leaving a faint red glow in the sky that would quickly fade to black.

"I don't think it's a good idea to risk driving back to the mine after dark," she commented in a quiet tone to Mr. Straddler. "Better to stay in Chilpancingo overnight."

"Agreed," he said. Turning to the brigadier general and appealing to his sense of playing the host in his city, she asked if he could recommend a hotel.

"Of course. We will make all of the necessary arrangements." As Chilpancingo was subject to violent clashes and organized crime movements, Aline wanted to maintain a low profile. However, there was little chance of that as they were escorted down the main avenue to the entrance of a small hotel by two military pickups with lights flashing and machine guns poised.

The guys turned in, and Aline decided to go out for a nightcap. On the main floor of the hotel, she spotted a cozy lounge and walked in, heading toward the bar to order a drink.

"Mojito, por favor."

"Claro que sí, señorita," said the bartender.

Waiting for her beverage, Aline took a seat and looked around, her eyes stopping at a table against the wall. It was the guy from the corner booth in La Katrina bar. He was with a female companion. She was slim and shapely with dark, long hair, wearing a skin-tight black dress and red stilettos that actually matched her lipstick. Both watched Aline attentively as the bartender placed her drink on a napkin in front of her. As she brought the glass up to her lips, the couple raised their drinks to her. She responded in kind with a smile.

Enjoying the ambiance, laid-back music, and two more *mojitos*, Aline got up. She needed to pee. Understandably wary of the bathrooms in Chilpancingo, she cautiously entered the tidy, well-lit restroom, crossed the floor, and took a seat in the farthest stall. A few moments later, someone came in and used the stall next to hers. Pulling up her panties and jeans, she flushed the toilet and adjusted her clothes. Unlatching the door, she took a few steps over to the marble sinks. The fixtures were golden and ornate, and the mirrors were large and elegantly framed. As the warm jet of water caressed her hands, the other occupant flushed the toilet and opened the stall door, stepping into view. It was the striking female from the table. She walked with poise to the sink next to Aline, meeting her glance in the mirror. Penetrating, obsidian-colored eyes, and a feline-esque shape. In an instant, Aline perceived a soft, clean, fresh scent exuding from the woman, which made her unintentionally inhale deeper, flooding her nostrils with the pleasant aroma.

“Hola,” said Aline politely. And before she could take another breath, the woman turned toward her and, drawing closer, stopped a few inches from Aline’s nose. The rousing fragrance now completely enveloped her mind and body. Aline’s pulse quickened, blood rushing to her head. She felt her lips swelling as she breathed through her mouth, her senses overloaded, lucidity sweeping into a haze of nothingness.

In one fluid motion, the woman brought her hands up, cupped the sides of Aline’s head, and pulled her in hard, thrusting her tongue deep inside of Aline’s open mouth. Aline felt the woman’s warm, moist saliva mix with hers.

“Mucho gusto. Soy Selene.”

CHAPTER 4

As of the PDAC convention in Toronto, an intricate political agenda was slowly coming into fruition. A formal letter had been sent to the president of Mexico authored by the president & CEO of the Company requesting government intervention with respect to the escalating security situation around its mines and projects. The Company was investing heavily in the country, creating jobs and sustainability beneficial to all stakeholders, both national and foreign, and the growing concern for employee safety and lack of demonstrated effect on the impetus of organized crime could incite the Company's board of directors to cease operations in the region and put into motion a divestment policy that would most likely be replicated by other mining companies.

The letter initiated a sequence of top-level meetings between the Company and the government, and Aline would be part of the diplomatic collective. First on the docket was a private audience with the secretary of the economy where the Company would present its petitions.

"Yeah, you know how lawyers are," said the senior vice president from the head office in an opening remark to the secretary of the economy. A narcissist extraordinaire, the SVP was known for his innate ability to put his foot in his mouth whenever possible. And he was managing to uphold his reputation.

"Well, yes I do," replied the government official lightheartedly. "I am a lawyer," he added, smiling politely. The political faux pas provoked a moment of uncomfortable silence, obliging the SVP to quickly make amends for his inappropriate comment. As was becoming a habit, Aline once again clamped down on her tongue with her teeth to stifle any outburst of laughter, which would probably not have been received too kindly. She took a sip of her cool water and for the moment put her mind somewhere else.

The Company wanted established military and/or law enforcement presence close to its mines that would theoretically act as a deterrent to organized crime. *After all, it could get pretty annoying to carry out executions, kidnappings, and extortions when you have the Federal Police, Army, or Navy in your backyard,* Aline reasoned.[22] The meeting came to a close, with a promise from the secretary that they would be contacted by the Ministry of the Interior to put a concrete plan into effect. Within a few days, the Company representatives—Mr. Bozeman, the VP of operations, the MGM from Guerrero, and Aline—were scheduled to meet the undersecretary of the Ministry to discuss the situation in greater detail.

The forum was official, with personalized nameplates printed neatly on white cardboard in

....

22 In recent years, the Navy, La Marina, has been at the forefront of military intervention against organized crime, carrying out unprecedented amounts of inland operations, countrywide.

front of twenty or so seats. The head of the table was reserved for the undersecretary. Coffee was served by uniformed staff while brief introductions were given by each person in attendance.

"Thank you, and welcome to the Ministry of the Interior," said the undersecretary in Spanish. "Let me begin by saying that communication between the public and private sectors is a priority for this administration, and meetings like this one are the result of our president's interest in promoting and fostering mutual collaboration."

Mr. Bozeman followed up in English with a statement of gratitude to the undersecretary and began with a slide presentation of the mining industry in Mexico—where the Company operates, its number of employees, and its volume of production. He waited patiently for the translation after each main point before continuing with the next. Meanwhile, Aline discreetly observed the participants around the table, jotting down specific little annotations of interest about each one into her black Moleskine notebook. Looking up, she noticed that the undersecretary was doing exactly the same thing, likewise detecting what Aline was doing, to which she gave him a tranquil smile. *Touché,* she thought, finding the shared surveillance tactic entertaining. The SVP finished his dissertation on mining and then brought up security, which was Aline's prompt to take out her folder and start citing specific, detailed incidents at the different mines.

The undersecretary, leaning forward in his chair and undoubtedly having planned far in advance what he was going to say next—at least in Aline's mind—

weighed in. "After considering what has been said, I believe that we can provide the Company with federal law enforcement presence through the use of our Federal Protection services."

There would be much ambiguity and confusion later concerning the concept of Federal Protection and what it really meant in terms of scope and its differentiation from Federal Police, not to mention the significant monetary cost that would be incurred to obtain this service. After some deliberation, Aline came up with her own definition of Federal Protection, which was especially useful when explaining it to the head office. Her description would eventually be accepted as the standard within the Company:

> Federal Protection is the private security of the Federal Government. It is not the Federal Police, even though they share the same uniforms, colors, logotypes, vehicles, and armament, only replacing the word "police" with "protection." Federal Protection is sanctioned to provide services only to mining and petroleum concessions, not other types of private business.

At the conclusion of the session, contact information was exchanged, and tentative dates were set for the next meeting.

"Mucho gusto, Señor Subsecretario," said Aline, shaking hands firmly with the official.

"Encantado, Señorita Aline."

CHAPTER 5

Late May, walking on the white-sand beach of the Fairmont Mayakoba in Playa del Carmen, the warm sand felt pleasant between Aline's toes. The Company's executive team was scheduled to participate in a series of regional meetings, including a crisis management training that Aline had effusively inserted into the agenda since there was a good chance that there would be future crises to attend to. She wanted to make sure that the team was prepared. She planned to conduct an intensive training session that included an introduction to the Company's Crisis Management Plan, the identification of team members and their roles and scope of responsibilities, and a real-time tabletop exercise.

A couple of hours before the training session began, Aline was sitting at breakfast, sipping her freshly squeezed grapefruit juice. She took in the salty air and contently flipped through the new and official Crisis Management Plan that she had personally structured, re-edited, and streamlined into a useful and applicable document. The original paper she had to work from was more than one hundred twenty pages in length and was laden with inconsistencies, anomalies, duplications, and errors that she found horribly painful and tedious to decipher. After months of steadily laboring away to perfect the plan and translate it into Spanish, she completed the job to the satisfaction of both her bosses and the head office.

Aline was well aware that most people—even security experts on occasion—found corporate security documents excruciatingly dull and almost unbearable, so she wanted to limit the theoretical part to a maximum of one hour, summarizing the key components in a presentation format with a few slides, colorful images and diagrams, limited text, and a short, amusing opening video concerning security perceptions portrayed by primates dressed as executives in a boardroom meeting.

Once everyone understood the content of the plan, Aline called for a ten-minute break to set up the parameters of the tabletop simulation. Prior to the training, she had prepared fictitious, sequential, and official-looking news releases concerning the kidnapping of a top-level Company official in the region, which her assistant would distribute as the situation unfolded. She orchestrated telephone calls from a distraught wife in Mexico City, recordings of the Company's president & CEO calling from Vancouver, which would be received in the conference room, and staged calls to the actual cell phone numbers of certain team members. The task of the CMT participants was to organize themselves, adopt their respective roles, set up a timeline of the incident, and carry out the plan accordingly.[23]

....

23 CMT—Crisis Management Team.

Aline was generally pleased with the results and how the team had handled the fictional crisis. Moreover, she was able to demonstrate that even though the incident had taken place in a controlled and sterile environment, two common errors that manifest perpetually during real-life crises had systematically surfaced: unchecked emotions that got the better of team members and a lack of effective communication, often influenced by precisely those same emotions, opinions, subjective beliefs, and outlooks. Aline had found that the most adequate and methodological approach to absolutely any type of crisis is to ask, "What do you know? What don't you know? What are you doing to find out?"

****

A double-crisis erupted in the Guerrero mine. About a week had passed since the session in Playa del Carmen. On the one hand, there was a work stoppage instigated by the labor union, which was apparently unsatisfied with the settlement amount reached during negotiations with the Company. They wanted an on-top sum or the strike would continue. On the other hand, community members, along with small children for added effect, blocked entry points and sections of the roadway leading to the mine, supposedly because the Company was not doing enough with respect to security in and around the mine. Whether the two situations were related, orchestrated by the same source, or happened to be a product of sheer coincidence was never confirmed, but the two groups seemed to fuse, which completely blurred the lines of where one began and the other ended.

In any case, by means of a few discreet chats with key internal and external persons, the root cause of the union's discontent was identified. The organized crime group in power was requesting—well, actually extorting—from the union a quota per worker, enforcing its demands with express-kidnappings, threats, and acts of violence. Since there was absolutely no way the Company would give in to this type of strong-arming, they opted to request an ad hoc meeting with the Ministry.

Over the next few days, there were discussions with the undersecretary regarding the ongoing critical situation. Because the labor dispute could be considered an internal Company issue, albeit influenced by an external criminal element, the meeting focused on the significant increase in violence around the Mezcala area. The ask from the Company was immediate law enforcement and/or military presence in the zone.

"I can assure you that we will take matters into our own hands," said the undersecretary to Mr. Bozeman.

"Thank you. We very much appreciate your support on this issue," he replied.

With the positive assurance from the Ministry, the SVP, the VP of operations, the MGM from the Guerrero mine, and Aline went out for a bite. During lunch, they wagered a beer over who could predict when they would receive some type of response from the authorities.

"Two days sounds right to me," said Mr. Bozeman. Aline estimated that before nightfall that very same day there would be some type of movement.

Sure enough, shortly after 6:00 p.m., a federal police Blackhawk helicopter made a number of low sweeps of the area. The protesters dispersed momentarily, unfortunately thinking that this was a ploy from the Company against them, when in fact, it was a message to the narcos in the area that the federal government was beginning to reclaim control in their territory.

By mid-June, Federal Protection services were permanently installed at the Guerrero mine; thirty-nine agents, uniformed and armed, patrolled the property 24/7.

Before month's end, Aline was back at the Mayakoba, this time for a series of leadership training sessions. A catamaran trip to a nearby reef for snorkeling only confirmed the arm's-length relationship between Aline and the sea.

"Man, I have to get off this ride or someone's gonna hurl. And that someone is going to be me," she laughed, green-faced with head spinning. The double dose of motion sickness medication was futile at best. "The power of Christ compels you," she said to herself, playing the scene from *The Exorcist* in her mind over and over, kneeling and slumped over the stern as fish gathered. Once back on solid ground, she gained her equilibrium—and color—and was ready for the evening's performance.

At about 3:00 p.m., the management team reconvened to receive the final instructions for the day.

"Everyone, if I can have your attention, please," said the organizer of the sessions. "This evening at 7:00 p.m., you will be hosting an event for approximately thirty people at the hotel, with music, wine, and food. This challenge will test each team's organizational and teamwork abilities. Good luck. The clock starts now."

"Okay. Let's divide up the tasks according to interests and abilities," said Mr. Johnnie from HR. A show of hands quickly followed to see who would be doing what as he rattled off a list of jobs.

"Music?" he continued.

Aline was an avid acoustic and electric guitar player, so she shot up her hand, as did the operations manager from the Guerrero mine, also an enthusiast. They united with the singing talents of the VP of operations to form a musical trio for the event. While the operations manager downloaded songs for the repertoire, Aline and the VP headed to the small town of Playa del Carmen to pick up some acoustic guitars. The Company's legal representative was tasked with food preparations, demonstrating her gastronomical prowess. Mr. Bozeman proudly and laughingly proclaimed that he had no skills or talent whatsoever in music, cooking, or mixing drinks. Therefore, he volunteered to take on the role of maître d' for the evening. He would welcome guests, show them to their tables, and ensure that things ran smoothly between the kitchen and dining room.

By 6:00 p.m., things were shaping up nicely. Aline was tuning guitars, reading over chords and lyrics, and doing a sound check on the audio system.

"Check one, two. Check one, two," she said into the mic.

The team staff bustled to and from the dining area located on an open-air but roofed patio. The "waiters" arranged plates, glasses, and colorful napkins. Menus that had been printed out were placed on tables, and a delicious aroma permeated from the kitchen.

The "band" managed to acquire hotel shirts, both for themselves and the waiters, and the whole team was good to go by the time the first guests arrived.

By evening's end, everyone was content that the soirée had turned out to be such a great success. Mr. Bozeman, standing by the table where his wife was seated, picked up his glass to make a toast. "Ladies and gentlemen, I just want to take this opportunity to say that I've worked with many people as part of a team over the span of my career, and I can honestly say that this group is above and beyond all of them. This exercise served as a demonstration of not only the team's ease in handling new challenges and their ability to work together on a common task under pressure, but also that they can have fun and really enjoy themselves. I'm proud to be a part of it. Here's to the Company's Mexico team."

"Cheers," everyone responded, raising their glasses.

CHAPTER 6

The regional rock star tour—as Aline colloquially referred to the intense, itinerary-packed mega-trips to all of the mines in one hit—was about to kick off, featuring Aline and her Canadian boss. The opening act was an NGO based out of Washington, D.C., which was commissioned to conduct an audit of the Company's mines in Mexico concerning the Voluntary Principles. The NGO's objective was to assess the actual situation at each site and provide basic training to key areas, such as security, human resources, and community relations.

As preparations for the tour were finalized, Aline was concerned about the ever-increasing risk level at the Guerrero mine. Another recent incident only confirmed it.

****

The office phone rang. Aline looked at the caller ID.

Ext. Security Office – Guerrero mine.

"Hola. ¿Cómo estás?" asked Aline, already knowing that something was up.

"Hola, Aline," said Joe. "I need to inform you of a situation that took place over the weekend that we were only now able to corroborate."

"Okay," she said, feeling her stomach tightening.

"During the weekend, an employee from the open pit decided that he would go to a local event to celebrate the fifteenth birthday of a girl from Carrizalillo." Aline had previously issued a regionwide communication stating that employees should not attend local nighttime events, particularly during the weekend, and especially if alcohol was served.

Joe continued. "At about 1:00 a.m., after consuming alcohol, most likely above the legal limit, he thought that it would be a good idea to go on a beer run, so he got into a car with a local and drove off, looking for more alcohol. As luck would have it, the vehicle was stopped at a false search and seizure point set up by a local crime group. Having no ID on his person, the armed group got hostile, and in a nervous, split-second decision, the employee bolted from the car in an attempt to escape, which ended with him being mowed down by machine-gun fire.

Aline knew the answer to her next question before she asked it.

"Did he survive the attack?"

"No. Dead on the spot."

"Shit. Okay. I need you to write it up so I can translate the report and send it to Corporate. Any chance it was linked to the Company?" she asked.

"No. These guys are usually stoned or seriously buzzing, and if anything suddenly goes down, they usually shoot first and ask questions later."

"All right. Thanks. If you receive any additional information, please let me know."

"Yes, of course."

Hanging up, Aline dialed Mr. Bozeman's office.

****

The next morning, Aline met with her boss and the NGO reps in front of the corporate office at the prearranged time. Shortly after, their trip to the Guerrero mine was underway.

"Everyone ready to go?" she asked.

"Ready as ever," responded the male representative. Aline sensed a twinge of nervousness in his voice.

The three-hour-forty-minute ride was uneventful, and the day filled up with meetings, classroom-type sessions, and general fact-finding rounds of the installations—all requirements of the NGO audit. In the afternoon, Aline received a call from the regional office requesting that she come back to Mexico City immediately for an urgent meeting with Federal Protection, which was scheduled early the following morning.

"Looks like I'll be catching up with you at the Chihuahua mine," she said to Mr. Straddler. She bid the group adieu and boarded the Company car that would take her back to Mexico City.

After the meeting with Federal Protection, the Company driver whisked her off to the international airport to catch her flight to Chihuahua. From Chihuahua, she boarded a single-engine Cessna—about the size of her Volvo S60—that would take her to the Chihuahua mine an hour away where she would once again rendezvous with the group.[24]

That evening after dinner, when Aline retired to her room, she reflected about the overall organized crime situation in Mexico, of course after checking her room extensively for possible noxious intruders. It was a forty- to sixty-billion-dollar, tax-free industry per year. Lucrative. And of course, enticing for the next generation of male youths—money, guns, alcohol, drugs, women, and above all, power. An expression that she had heard often while traveling through the northern states that always stuck in her mind and pretty much summed it up was: "I would prefer to live five years as a king than fifty as an ox."[25] *No argument there*, she thought.

The next day, they boarded the Cessna and left for the Zacatecas mine, about a three-hour flight away, stopping to refuel in Parral, Chihuahua. It was pretty tight in the aircraft, and Aline questioned if it could handle the human cargo and gear. She sat in the copilot's seat, with her knees high up toward her body to avoid bumping into any controls inadvertently.

"How would you describe daily life in the Chihuahua mine, with such a ubiquitous presence of organized crime in the region and no law enforcement or military to fall back on?" asked one of the NGO reps.

"Coexistence," said Aline with a bit of irony. "You know, something along the lines of, 'Hello, Mr. Drug

24 The Company eventually stopped using single-engine aircraft per flight safety protocol in regard to flying in and out of the mines.

25 The Spanish phrase is: *"Prefiero vivir cinco años como rey que cincuenta como buey."*

Lord. How are things?' 'Fine thanks. How's production?' 'Good. And you?' 'Good.' 'Okay. Bye now. Have a nice day.' But on a more serious note," she said, "recently, we had forty to sixty heavily armed men come to one of the gates requesting passage across the mine property, their pickups laden with harvested product, as their usual route was blocked by a rival group, a rival group that also happens to control the road to Choix, Sinaloa."

"Bummer," retorted Mr. Straddler sarcastically.

"Of course, the request was more of a rhetorical question than anything else. The answer would be yes or yes. There was no way in hell that mine security, though armed with assault rifles, could handle that number of hopped-up, prone-to-violence, trigger-happy, exalted thugs. They were outmanned and outgunned. Pretty obvious how things would play out."

Aline waited for the follow-up question, which she knew would never come, but she imagined it anyway: "So, just to get a better understanding of the situation, by allowing the group, who has most likely violated a human right or two at one time or another, to cross the mine property with illegal weapons and drugs, isn't the Company violating the Voluntary Principles...and the law?" Silence. Only the hum of the aircraft's engine.

As they neared Parral, Aline thought to herself, *Shouldn't have drunk so much coffee.* She urgently needed a bio-break. Landing, she quickly exited the aircraft in search of a loo. A soldier approached to register their names on the clipboard he carried.

"Is there a washroom here?" she asked desperately.

"Um. Don't know," he replied. Aline gave him a clear WTF expression as she turned her back on him and headed toward some buildings. Right on the button. She found a small kitchen-cafeteria with restrooms.

After a while, they sat down to eat some homemade breakfast, and then they picked up the journey where they had left off, boarding the aircraft again.

The head of site security was already at the airstrip when they landed in Cedros, Zacatecas, with two pickups at the ready. Aline rode with him while his 2 I/C drove Mr. Straddler and the NGO reps.

"What's new?"

"Yesterday, one of our female security personnel detected and confiscated a block of cyanide from an employee leaving the mine."[26]

"That's very concerning," she said. "If the intention was to dump the block into a water supply, that could have had a serious impact on the local population and the Company in terms of liability." Aline thought for a minute. "Are there still rumors of clandestine meth labs north of Concepcíon de Oro?" she asked.

"Come to think of it, yes. Why do you ask?"

"Well, apparently cyanide is one of about four hundred compounds that can be used in the production of methamphetamine. I need you to investigate and find out what the end purpose for the block was, okay?"

"Got it."

****

In recent months, Aline had been invited by the president of the Canadian Chamber of Commerce in

....

26 Cyanide was packaged in one-kilogram blocks and utilized in the Heap Leach Pad process.

Mexico to chair its security committee. She recalled the pleasant chat that she had with the president of the Chamber, who was also Canadian and an expatriate from the city of Ottawa.

"The idea is that you head up the security group and use the forum to exchange pertinent information with the heads of security of different Canadian companies operating in the region, not to mention liaising with the embassy, their security section, and the ambassador herself."

"It really sounds like an interesting initiative, and I am honored to have been nominated," she said.

"Well, we're excited to have you onboard, as part of CANCHAM."

****

The incoming phone call was from an external number.

"¿*Sí*. Buenos días?"

"Buenos días. May I please speak to Aline Belanger?" said a pleasant female voice.

"Yes, this is she. Who may I ask is calling?"

"This is the office of the Canadian ambassador in Mexico. The ambassador would like to invite you to a petit comité at the Four Seasons Hotel next month to chat with investors and company heads from a number of Canadian financial institutions interested in conducting business in the country."

"That sounds wonderful. Thank you very much."

"Great. I will send you the formal invitation, and I would request that you RSVP as soon as possible."

"Absolutely. Thank you again, and have a nice day."

The Four Seasons, as per reputation, was elegant and proper with courteous staff who received and escorted Aline to the private dining room that had been reserved for the ambassador. Cell phone in hand, she noted that she had no bars. *Odd. Was the interference caused by the structure of the hotel itself or a deliberate signal jammer?* she thought as she observed various Mexican government EP personnel lurking in the vicinity of their principal.[27] The room was quaint with elegant decor, and the table was set with eight chairs, four on one side, three on the other, and one at the head.

"Buenos días, Señorita Belanger," said the ambassador's aide.

"Buenos días."

"The Ambassador will be here shortly, as well as the other invitees. Please have a seat."

"Gracias."

"Buenos días, señorita. ¿Jugo de naranja o toronja?" asked a uniformed waiter.

"Toronja, por favor."

After a few minutes, the ambassador walked in, followed by five gentlemen—two Mexican nationals and three foreigners, who were easily identifiable as the Canadians based on their friendly and higher-than-normal level of politeness. Aline almost hoped that one of them was carrying a concealed package of Timbits.[28]

"Good morning, everyone. Please take your seats," said the ambassador. Tall and fair-skinned with

....

27 Principal–Term used in executive protection to signify the VIP that is being protected.

28 Timbits–Delicious bite-sized morsels from the Canadian doughnut franchise, Tim Hortons.

straight blonde hair and blue eyes, she had an air of kindness about her. "Why don't we go around the table to introduce ourselves?"

Assuming that she would say a few words about herself, Aline was pleasantly surprised when the ambassador actually made a small introduction for each person.

"And to my left is Aline Belanger, Canadian national and Regional Director of Security for the Company, with many years of security experience and know-how in Mexico." *Impressive, thought Aline.*

After the intros, the waiters served breakfast. One of the Canadian bankers turned to Aline and asked, "What would you consider to be an effective security strategy for a foreign company with operations in Mexico?"

She put down her fork from her half-eaten quiche, eloquently wiping the corners of her mouth with a napkin, and said, "The objective of any security strategy should be to navigate the complexity of the situation while making your company less attractive to the criminals. It should not be to dismantle, confront, or give in to the demands of Organized Crime. If the state of affairs is already complicated, then add on to that complexity, which creates conditions for a company to get lost in the shuffle and blend in."

The banker nodded his head. "Please continue."

"The approach should not be focused on problem-solution thinking. That would be a truly disheartening one-way ticket to failure. Instead, you need to focus on generating numerous alternatives to confuse, misdirect, and/or frustrate the criminal element, which will most likely make them look elsewhere. One instance comes to mind. About two months back, a small group of armed local thugs, most likely related to one of the organized crime groups or one of their factions operating in the area, approached the main gate of our mine in Guerrero and insisted on speaking with the owner of the Company."

Aline recalled how the situation unfolded.

"Sí," said the leader of the group to the security officer. "We would like to talk with the person in charge."

"Disculpe, señor," said the guard as part of his learned dialogue. "There is no owner here at the mine." Using everyday terms, he explained that the Company was publicly traded, so there was no one owner and that the main office was far off to the north, somewhere in Canada. "There are only miners here," he continued.

The leader of the group paused for a moment, confused, apparently trying to assimilate the information that he had just received, and then he carried on. "Okay, then just show us where the lingotes are," he said, referring to the gold bullion.

"I'm sorry," replied the officer. "But there are no gold bars on the property, only ore concentrate and doré bars that need refining, and that is a very complicated process."

"By this time, the group was getting nowhere," Aline explained, "so they eventually decided to leave on their own. And this is just one example of educating the bad guys. Mix into the complexity of the situation armed Federal Protection, Auxiliary State Police, a specialized task force, and customized security measures all under the aegis of intelligence-driven security, and voilà! You have a security formula with a good chance of being very successful."

"That's pretty amazing, Aline," said the ambassador.

"Thank you," she said. "To date, it has given us positive results. I would only add that you need to be flexible, always adapting to the ever-changing security landscape. There really is no one singular, concrete solution for insecurity in Mexico," she said. "Well, maybe one." Aline paused for effect. "Don't do business in Mexico." Her comment was met with laughter all around. "But seriously, you can have profitable and sustainable ventures here. You just need to be smart about it."

****

Almost one year had passed since Aline had stepped onto the high-octane, adrenaline-pumping, head-spinning roller coaster ride of security in the mining industry of Mexico. Drinking a coffee in the executive VIP lounge of the private hangars of the Toluca Airport, she popped a Gravol pill just in case there was too much turbulence on the small Company aircraft while flying to Zacatecas. She was accompanying the MGM from Guerrero to a meeting with the state secretary of economic development to discuss the security situation and other matters impacting the Zacatecas mine.

"That's correct, Mr. Secretary," said the MGM. "We really need your help and support in terms of security to make sure that the Company can keep contributing to the economy by creating new jobs and advancing social programs in the state's rural areas, which would also allow us to continue making donations to the governor's worthy and respectable causes." *Now that was a political mouthful,* thought Aline. *And there's nothing like throwing in a subtle allusion to a quid pro quo.*

One week later, sitting at her desk on a rainy day in Mexico City, Mr. Bozeman called her into his office.

"Hi, Aline. Come on in."

"What's up?" she asked.

"Well, my boss in Vancouver is leaving the Company, and the board informed me that as of September first, I'm being promoted to the position of executive vice president and chief operating officer of the Company."

"Wow!" It was really the only word that came out of Aline's mouth. In that same moment, she thought that this must have been an extremely emotional time for him. His dad had just passed away, and now his corporate career was taking the next step.

Aline felt a bittersweet emotion welling up inside of her. "You know, I have to tell you that I consider you to be the best boss that I have ever had, and I'm really sad and truly sorry to see you go. That said, I am elated that you have achieved such a high-standing position within the Company. Kudos to you."

"Thank you, Aline. It was a pleasure working with you," said Mr. Bozeman, extending his hand. The quiet, confident straight shooter from Montana born to a miner's family would soon depart and be replaced by another miner, this time from Chile.

By mid-autumn, Aline was discussing the integration plan for Federal Protection services with management on-site at the Zacatecas mine. The boardroom was spacious and somewhat dark, with a large mahogany-looking table and comfortable leather chairs around it.

"But how do we know if Federal Protection is really the right choice for our mine?" asked the manager of the Controlling Department haughtily.

Listen, lady, which part of the introductory remarks concerning the Corporate mandate to implement Federal Protection at the mine didn't you understand? That was what Aline wanted to say, but instead she opted to respond politely. "The idea is to replicate what we did at the Guerrero mine with respect to the installation of Federal Protection, and as I mentioned at the beginning of the meeting, this is coming down from the head office, so we need to make sure that we take care of it tout suite."

In less than a month's time, with air miles adding up, Aline returned to Zacatecas via Monterrey, Nuevo León, along with two Federal Protection agents commissioned to conduct a risk assessment of the mine. The assessment was a preliminary requirement for rendering services. By October, FP was up and running alongside the existing security guard service.[29]

****

"So, tell me again what actually transpired with the agents?" Aline asked the head of security. Not more than a month had gone by since the contract was signed with Federal Protection when the Company had its first major hiccup with the service.

29 It was erroneously rumored at the Zacatecas mine that Federal Protection was actually the private army of Aline Belanger and that there never was any indication from corporate headquarters to implement the service.

"Last Saturday, after ending their morning shift, a few agents decided to partake in a soccer game with Municipal Police," he said. "Following the match, they went to a local bar where they started to drink, which apparently carried over into the evening. As expected, the agents got into a verbal argument with the locals, which escalated into a bar brawl." *Great. Another case of chronic stupidity,* Aline thought.

"But it didn't end there," continued the head of security. "After some of the locals left the establishment, the agents hooked up with Municipal Police, who had also been drinking, and decided to take matters into their own hands by searching out the offenders. They identified the home of one of the wrongdoers, and the agents kicked down the front door and dragged him out into the street for a light pistol-whipping as his pregnant wife stood in the doorway in utter dismay."

"Unbelievable," Aline said, shaking her head. "Have the agents been removed from active duty?"

"If you mean are they still working at the mine? No. Their supervisor took them off the work roster, and I haven't seen them since."

"And do you know if they've been suspended or dismissed from Federal Protection?"

"No idea."

"Looks like I'll be visiting the Federal Protection offices in Mexico City when I get back."

****

"Adelante." "Buenos días, Aline," said Joe L. from the Guerrero mine. "We have another apparent secuestro to deal with." It was about noon on Wednesday.

"Okay. What do we know at present?"

"A doctor on staff was apparently abducted early this morning around 6:00 a.m. when he was leaving from his girlfriend's house for work in the locality of Sabana Grande. He was supposedly intercepted by two armed men on foot who forced him into his own vehicle and then drove off." *I'm glad that he's finally adopted the proper use of words to describe the incident. Good for him,* she thought.

"Has there been a ransom demand made?"

"Yes. According to his family, the kidnappers are evidently asking five hundred thousand pesos for his return."

"Any indication that it is related to the Company?"

"Well, the girlfriend mentioned that when the kidnappers first approached and pointed their guns at them, one of them had asked the other if it was him, and he answered, 'Yeah, that's him. He's the doctor from the Company.'"

"Okay. Good job on the preliminary information gathering. Try to maintain continuous communication with the family. Also, do you know the girlfriend?" she asked.

"No. Only that she's an employee of the mine, but the coronel does."

"Okay. Have him contact her and follow up to see if he can substantiate anything else while I inform Top Management and Corporate Security. I'll call you back in half an hour."

Aline hung up and dialed Mr. Straddler.

"Oh, hey Aline. What's up?" he asked.

"The doctor from the Guerrero mine has been kidnapped, and it may have something to do with the Company," she said, continuing to brief him on the details.

"Okay. I'll inform the London Desk, and—"

"Hold on," Aline interrupted. "Joe L. is calling me, probably with an update."

"Go ahead," said Mr. Straddler.

"Aline. The coronel just got off the phone with the girlfriend, and she said that she also remembered hearing the kidnapper in charge, the one who had asked about the doctor, say that the pinche Compañía was stealing gold from the people of Guerrero."

"Okay, Joe. Thanks. Please keep me posted. I have Mr. Straddler on the other line."

"Enterado," said Joe.

"So, what did he say?" asked Mr. Straddler.

"He said that one of the kidnappers had also made a comment about the Company, that they were stealing gold from the people of Guerrero."

"Hmm. Sounds like it might be Company related after all. I'll call London and request they be on standby."

On Thursday afternoon, they spoke again.

"Any proof of life that the doctor is still alive?" asked Mr. Straddler.

"No," said Aline. "Nothing. All we have is that the family is still negotiating with the kidnappers for his release."

"All right. Well, the London Desk informed me that the earliest they could get one of their K&R specialists to Mexico is late tomorrow night. I commented that you could receive them in the regional office early Saturday morning."

"Absolutely. You can count on me."

The next morning, Aline spoke again with Joe L.

"Aline. We were just informed that the doctor has been released," he said.

"That's great news. How is he?"

"Dehydrated and pretty beat-up. His family is taking him to the Hospital Royal Care in Iguala."

"Okay. I want you to head out to the hospital and talk to the physician in charge about his actual status, then see when it would be appropriate for you to debrief him."

It was Saturday morning, and since it was the weekend, the main entrance to the corporate building where the Company's regional office was housed was closed, and all authorized persons entering needed to do so from the service entrance. Aline waited patiently near the building's security control room for the specialist from London and the local host, John, whom she already knew from the K&R service.

"Morning, Aline. Nice to see you again," said John.

"You too," she said, shaking hands with him.

"I'd like you to meet our specialist from London."

"Nice to meet you, sir."

"Likewise, I'm sure."

"Why don't we head to my office?" Aline suggested.

Once they settled into the office, the specialist asked, "So, what do we have, Aline?"

"Well, as I mentioned over the phone when you landed in Mexico, the doctor has been released and is currently in a hospital in Iguala, Guerrero."

"How is he?" asked John.

"Physically, he's okay. Dehydrated, and he sustained a number of injuries during the ordeal, particularly on his feet since the kidnappers took his shoes when they released him. He told my superintendent of security this morning that he was let go in a mountainous area and had to walk approximately ten kilometers to get home."

"Good to hear that he's generally all right," said the specialist. "The plan is that I head out to the hospital and get a formal statement from him and try to ascertain, per insurance protocol, whether the kidnapping had something to do with the Company or not."

"What about the ransom, Aline?" inquired John.

"All we know is that the family carried out a payment in an undisclosed amount." Aline looked directly at the specialist. "Do you speak any Spanish?"

"No. Unfortunately, not a word," he replied in a very pronounced British accent. *So, how are you planning on getting a statement from the doctor?* Aline considered saying. Instead, she replied, "That could be a bit complicated because the doctor, as I understand, does not speak English, nor does my superintendent or his second-in-command. Meanwhile, have you made the arrangements for getting to Iguala?" she asked, almost knowing the forthcoming answer.

"No. Do you have any suggestions?" he asked. *I can see that the Company's money was well spent on the service...or not. I mean, sure they are subject-matter experts—there's no doubt there—but how do you neglect basic planning logistics while sending someone who doesn't speak the language? Mind-boggling.*

"Well, if you are in agreement, I can have the team leader from our local task force in Guerrero meet you at the Iguala toll booth, and from there he can take you to the hospital and also act as a translator. You would only need to take an authorized taxi from here."

"Smashing, Aline. Thank you very much for the support."

"No problem. The team leader is a big, muscular lad with light hair, a Hungarian chap who speaks English and Spanish. You should be able to identify him quickly enough. And once I have confirmation of the vehicle he will be using to pick you up and the plates, I will text them to you."

Monday morning. Aline audibly sighed.

"Did you see the report that the K&R specialist sent?" asked Aline. She had called Mr. Straddler first thing.

"Hold on. Let me open up my e-mail," he answered sleepily on the phone. "Let me see. Dah da da da dah... and the conclusion of the debriefing with the doctor at the Hospital Royal Care in Iguala, Guerrero would indicate that the kidnapping was not in any way or form related to or directed at the Company. The abduction originally started out as a carjacking against the doctor, whom the perpetrators had only identified as being an employee of the mine. Unbelievable," he said.

"Yup. Welcome to Mexico," Aline added.

****

Before the year's end, a curious incident played out involving the niece of a colleague from one of the mines. The girl was an art student specializing in the restoration of paintings.

"Hey. What are you doing here in the regional office?" she asked her colleague, smiling.

"Just a couple meetings with my boss. Can I talk to you for a minute?"

"Sure. Come on in."

"Thanks," he said, closing the door behind him. "I wanted to tell you about an incident that happened last week to my niece, who studies at a university in Guanajuato."

"Okay."

"After finishing her last class in the afternoon, she was kidnapped by a number of men who forced her into a van where they blindfolded her."[30]

"Please go on," said Aline, writing down what she was hearing.

"She told me that she didn't know exactly how long they had driven, maybe thirty minutes. When the van finally stopped, they took her out of the vehicle and removed her blindfold. That was when she became aware that she was in a small clearing, and there was a helicopter making a lot of noise. Loose grass and dirt were flying all over the place from the rotor blade. Two men in dark suits stepped out and approached her, then grabbed her arms and walked her back to the chopper. The blindfold was put on again, and they flew her to an unknown location. For the next three days, she was given the task of restoring various works of art that she easily identified as two Picassos and a Rembrandt."

"Wow, that's really incredible."

"It is," he remarked. "She said that they gave her food and water, and once her work was completed,

30 In the strictest sense, this was not considered kidnapping since no ransom was requested. This would be classified as the illegal privation of a person's liberty.

she was again blindfolded and flown back to the original starting point and given five hundred pesos as taxi fare."

"Well, looking on the bright side, even though it must have been a harrying experience, she made it out alive and unscathed."

"Yeah. That's what I told her. Aline, do you think they specifically targeted my niece, or were they just looking for an art student?" he asked worriedly.

"To tell you the truth, it's most likely that they had been monitoring her for a while, maybe using someone to identity the senior students of the art program and ask around in terms of who were the best and most apt students."

"What makes you say that?"

"Well, if you think about it, these criminals had possession of stolen famous paintings that are undoubtedly worth a hefty price, and they wouldn't risk having them damaged by some first-year art student."

"I guess that sounds logical," he said, gazing out for a moment and then looking up. "Do you think they'll look for her again?" he asked, concerned for his niece's well-being.

"You know, it is possible since they already know how she works and where she studies, and if they happen to come upon other stolen artwork that needs restoration, they would definitely be interested in finding her. I would strongly recommend changing schools and even studying out of state. Even though it would be somewhat of a hassle, I think that it is in her best interest."

****

As the new year rolled in, due to the increasingly unstable security situation in Guerrero, Aline emitted a company-wide restriction for all ground travel to and from the mine, particularly for persons traveling from the regional office in Mexico City, visitors, expats, and employees who lived in Cuernavaca, Morelos. Air travel only.

This worked out quite well, as construction of the new airstrip located on-site and within the perimeter of the mine was finalized and ready for use.[31] Aline also made sure to include two small but substantial details at the end of the document: the signature of the regional SVP, the boss of everyone's boss, and a disclaimer stating that anyone not abiding by the restriction would be subject to disciplinary action and/or dismissal from the Company.

Arriving at the Cuernavaca airport, Aline made her way to a private hangar and had a coffee while waiting for the flight crew to arrive. The trip was short, approximately thirty-two minutes from takeoff to landing. As they approached the mine, she could hear the pilot communicating with security personnel on standby on the ground. After the aircraft landed and came to a complete stop, the captain got out and opened the door. A hot gust of tropical air enveloped her as she walked to the guardhouse to register. She shook hands with Joe L., and they boarded the vehicle that would take her to the mine.

The recently implemented ban served to mitigate the risk of road travel over longer distances. However,

....

31 The primary aircraft utilized here were the Company's King Air, Twin Otter, and Dash 8, with a maximum capacity of thirty-nine passengers.

it was totally inapplicable with respect to the daily necessity of driving to and from different mine locations, such as the canteen and employee campground, which were connected by one public roadway. To remedy the matter, vehicular convoys were put into effect.

"Why don't you tell me about the logistics of the convoys, Joe?"

"Sure. At designated times throughout the day, one police pickup with lights flashing leads the employee transport fleet, and another brings up the rear in a procession of eight to ten vehicles." The objective was plain and simple: Avoid being mistaken for narcos, particularly when the mine pickups are coincidentally similar—four-door Hemi engine trucks with polarized glass and big rims. Aline would later address this issue, slowly replacing vehicles in the fleet with smaller, less powerful two-door pickups that were less likely to be mistaken for rival crime groups. The macho narcos wouldn't be caught dead in such puny vehicles, not to mention the annoying matter of not being able to fit their crews inside with their awkward and bulky AK-47 assault rifles.

In the afternoon, Aline boarded the outgoing flight to Cuernavaca, then snoozed during the hour-and-a-half drive to Mexico City. The catnap served its purpose, as she was roused at 1:15 a.m. by a call on her cell phone.

"Hello?" she asked groggily.

"Aline? It's Rafa from the IT Department.

"What's up?"

"I just got off the phone with my boss's father, Jimmy's dad." Jimmy was a young manager with whom Aline had often chatted. "He told me that earlier tonight, Jimmy had been assaulted, and in the process, was shot and killed."

"How did it happen?" Aline asked.

"He was sitting in the car with his girlfriend when two armed assailants attempted to carjack the vehicle. Apparently, he refused and made an effort to drive off, when one of the guys shot him in the neck."

"Do we know where it happened?"

"Yes. In Iztapalapa. Qué mal," she said.[32]

"Okay. Thank you for the information, Rafa. I will inform the regional SVP and human resources," said Aline, hanging up. "Qué en paz descansa."

****

By the end of the month, Aline was off to the mine in the northwest, staying overnight at the Wingate Hotel in Chihuahua. Before turning in, she thought about the pros and cons of Federal Protection, which had been installed in two of the three operations in Mexico. Specifically, what potential threats and risks might the employees at the Chihuahua mine be subject to if the Company was seen as the entity that brought a federal law enforcement agency into the area? The FP agents would, of course, have to be flown in and out of the mine; any intention of driving a police vehicle toward Choix, Sinaloa or Chihuahua would be extremely ill-advised and short-lived. And it would be nearly impossible to try and contract enough federal agents to counter the number of armed narcos in the region. She

32 Iztapalapa—One of Mexico City's sixteen boroughs, it is known for its violence and criminal activity.

fell asleep with the idea that Federal Protection would probably not work on this occasion.

William, the MGM of the Chihuahua mine, was American. He was an older gentleman, calm and thoughtful, who commuted from his home in Phoenix, Arizona once a week via King Air or Twin Otter, depending on availability.

"Hello, Aline. How have you been?" he asked.

"Fine thanks. How about yourself? How's Arizona?"

"Dry as usual," he chortled. "Come on in, and let's chat."

They sat together for quite some time discussing Federal Protection, and both of them came to the conclusion that it would be far too risky to bring them in.

"So we agree?" he asked.

"Absolutely, William. Now we just need to adjust the security strategy for the mine." The inherited and actual conundrum they found themselves in was that the security guards on-site armed with 7.62mm assault rifles exclusive to the military and law enforcement were contracted through a third-party, private-security provider located in Chihuahua, and the only way to carry the firearms was to have personnel registered as official Municipal Police, which they were. The quid pro quo between the Company and the municipality took the following form: The Company "purchased" the firearms from the municipality on the condition that the weapons would be limited to the services of the mine, and monthly "salaries" would be paid out to Municipal Police by the Company. Once the mine was closed, the weapons would be returned to the municipality.

"Man, nothing like backdoor arrangements," said Aline.

"Sorry. That was something my predecessor had agreed to. I suppose it doesn't make sense to change it right now."

"No, it doesn't. Other than the fact that you would be exposing the mine as a soft target with no armed security personnel, you would also be adding another enemy to the list if you cut off the payroll of the Municipal Police."

"Why don't we put the item on hold temporarily?"

"Agreed."

****

Aline was back in Playa del Carmen, this time at the Grand Velas Riviera Maya Resort for the second part of the leadership training program. The setting was unsurprisingly enchanting, with its lush, tropical flora, well-kept areas, and hospitable staff. The resort was distributed over a significant piece of elongated real estate, so roofed golf carts were used to transport guests from one place to another. There were also bicycles at strategic points for anyone to use in case there was no cart in sight.

In the late afternoon, Aline decided to go for a walk on the beach. She always tried to make the effort to do so whenever she had the opportunity to be near the ocean. Waiting good-naturedly for the last cart of the day to the beach, she stood in the shade of a group of palm trees and watched small lizards darting from cover to cover. After a few minutes, she could hear the unmistakable hum of a golf cart drawing near.

"Buenas tardes, señorita. ¿Va a la playa?" asked the driver courteously.

"Sí, muchas gracias."

That evening, she reviewed a recently conducted analysis concerning potential hub cities that could optimize travel logistics to and from the mines. "Looks like the largest volume of people is clearly traveling to the Zacatecas mine via the City of Zacatecas to the southwest," she commented to herself. She decided that this would be the focal point of her next initiative.

Aline conceptualized the notion of a mini task force, a small group of armed and specially trained personnel stationed in the city that would be responsible for daily monitoring and reporting on the security climate. Since the team would be working out of Zacatecas, they would also have the capability of extending its services to cover Monterrey, Nuevo León in the northeast. She envisioned the task force establishing police contacts in the area and providing direct support for VIP visits, including accompaniment and security advance party, or SAP, duties. "Works for me," she said, feeling satisfied with her idea.

The only remaining question was who could provide such a security team. Aline jogged her memory for business contacts and came up with a friend that had worked at another German automaker. Even though they had not been in contact for years, she called him up.

"Amigo. ¿Cómo has estado? Soy Aline," she said cheerfully.

"Hola, amiga. ¿Bien, y tú? Qué milagro. ¿Qué hay?"

"Everything's great. I'm currently head of regional security for the Company."

"Guau. I'm sure that's a challenge for you, but I'm also sure that if anyone can handle it, it's you."

"Gracias, my friend. I was wondering if you knew of anyone trustworthy, discreet, and competent who could provide me with specialized security services."

"Por supuesto. I know of a couple of Israeli brothers who I have worked with on several occasions with positive results. They have a small company in Mexico City. I'll send you their contact information, and you can tell them that I sent you."

"Perfecto. Muchísimas gracias. Let's have lunch sometime soon, my treat."

"*Órale*. Me parece muy bien. Un abrazo."

****

By late February, Aline returned to the Guerrero mine to participate in a private on-site meeting with the MGM and community members from Mezcala. As she looked around the conference room table, she noted general concern on the faces of the local people. The item of discussion was the increasing level of insecurity in the vicinity of the town.

"Ingeniero," said the group leader, who happened to be the mayor's brother, "thank you for receiving us in your busy schedule."

"No thanks are required," answered the MGM. "It is always a pleasure to chat with the people of Mezcala. We consider ourselves your neighbors." *Nice. If mining doesn't work out for the MGM, then I'm sure that he can easily find a posting in local politics.* "So, how may we be of assistance to you?" continued the MGM.

"Thank you for asking. As you know, the security situation in our town has been deteriorating lately, and we wanted to know what the Company can do for us."

Aline's first thought was that the Company was neither law enforcement nor the armed forces; it had absolutely no authority to intervene in public security. She surmised that the request was based on the fact that the community was obviously aware of the Federal Protection services installation at the mine and perhaps thought that this "police force" could do something in the area.

"I imagine that you have seen that there are, in fact, new Federal Protection officers protecting the installations," said the MGM.

"Actually, yes. We were very surprised to see them."

"Are they Federal Police?" asked the chief of the Municipal Police.

"No. They are Federal Protection agents."

"Ahh," the chief answered, evidently confused. "And when can they start patrolling the streets of Mezcala?"

"Unfortunately, they are contractually bound to provide services only within the mine," said Aline. "Any action or posture on their behalf outside of the Company could expose the mine to significant threats and risks."

"Then what are we supposed to do about the criminals in our town?" countered one of the delegates.

"We can only recommend that you report the incidents to the authorities as soon as they occur so they can attend to the situation as needed," responded the MGM. *Not too comforting,* thought Aline. But those were the facts. Neither the Company nor any service provided to them could enforce the law in Mezcala.

As the dialogue continued, one of the community leaders, who was frustrated because they weren't getting anywhere with their original objectives, inadvertently blurted out that they had previously carried out a payment to the criminal group in power for protection services. *Pandora's box,* thought Aline. *One sole exhibition of payment to Organized Crime would turn into an unending practice.* As Aline would soon find out, the new drug lord of the region, El Líder, was indeed looking to the communities for economic support.

In the late afternoon, Aline was sitting at a small table in front of a local place that served coffee when an armored Audi A8 with polarized glass pulled up, and the driver's side window came down.

"Sube," said the man she recognized from the hotel lounge in Chilpancingo. She hesitated momentarily, then left a twenty-peso bill on the table and got in.

"How have you been?" he asked.

"Pretty good, thanks, and you?" Aline answered, casually noticing a gold-plated pistol peering out from under the man's belt buckle—a .38 Super, the preferred narco handgun.

"Selene sends her regards." Aline felt her face flush. It was a good thing she was wearing sunglasses so he wouldn't be able to see her pupils dilating.

"Thanks," she said. As they drove on, she candidly asked, "¿Cómo te llamas?"

"They call me Teniente," he answered dryly. "¿Y tú?"

"I'm Aline."

"Mucho gusto," he said, relaxing somewhat. "You remember La Katrina?"

"Yes, of course." *How could I forget?*

"You handled yourself quite well in the bathroom. My men still have scars to remind them of you," he smirked.

Perplexed, she turned and looked at him. "What do you mean, your men?"

"Yes. They are my socios—my business associates. I asked them to follow you to see what you would do."

A bit miffed, Aline played with the idea of punching him in the side of the neck, but he might lose control of the vehicle, so she refrained.

"Let me explain," he continued. "I could see when you walked into the bar that you could handle yourself. I just wanted to make sure for myself. I need someone like you in my organization, and I can offer you ten times what the mining company is paying you. By the way, what do you do there? Dig for gold?" he laughed.

Thinking quickly, she responded, "Maintenance. I make sure that all of the parts of the SAG mill are functioning optimally."[33] She didn't want to say something like "geologist" because she might have been asked to explain the difference between a rock and a stone.

"Sounds exciting," he said sarcastically.

"Where are we going?" she asked.

"A little place of mine with great entertainment in Tixtla. Are you up for it?"

....

33 SAG Mill—Semi-Autogenous Grinding Mill. A mill that uses steel balls, in addition to large rocks, for grinding materials from large chunks into small, usable pieces for processing.

"Okay." She knew that they were driving in the direction of Chilpancingo and would shortly be turning east.

By the time they arrived, it was already dark. *Un table,* she thought as they pulled up to the adult bar. A muscle-bound guy at the door greeted them with a nod as they went in. It was a smoke-filled space with blaring music and totally nude dancers on tables and in the laps of paying customers. Everywhere she looked were assault rifles and pistols, and it seemed that some of the patrons were doing lines of cocaine mixed with some sort of dark, powder-like substance with tightly rolled five-hundred-peso bills. *Nasty,* she thought.

They got to the VIP section—if you could call it that in this establishment—and Aline recognized the red high heels attached to the slender and well-formed naked body dancing on the table. *Selene.*

"Please sit down, and let's have some drinks," said Teniente.

Sunrise. Head spinning. Hair and clothes reeking of smoke, sweat, and alcohol. *Too much liquor. At least I stayed away from the powder and don't seem to have acquired any tattoos,* she justified. Stepping out into the daylight, Aline fumbled desperately for her sunglasses. Finding them, she staggered to the Audi. *Ready to go back to your exciting job?*

****

Adding to the instability of the zone and the entire state of Guerrero was the emergence of various armed auto-defense groups—a.k.a. rural and/or community "police"—as a result of the shared perception that the federal government was having little to no effect in deterring the violence perpetuated by Organized Crime. The groups were made up of persons from the respective municipalities under the "mandate" of protecting themselves in the interest of their communities.

Unfortunately, the groups in general were nothing more than vigilantes taking the law into their own hands and carrying out the same type of violent acts that they were supposedly trying to halt. Moreover, it was never ascertained who was actually funding the impoverished rural police, who were often in possession of costly, state-of-the-art, high-powered firearms exclusive to military use. Aline theorized that the financial backing in question could have originated from the organized crime groups themselves operating in the area in an attempt to oust rivals, or perhaps funding came from one the leftist political parties trying to destabilize the current government.

****

"Close your eyes and breathe deeply, inhaling through the nose and exhaling through the mouth," said the tall, slim instructor from Uruguay as he passed around the circle of seated practitioners, stopping at each one to trace imperceptible symbols above their heads. Aline felt herself drifting placidly from one thought to the next, listening to soft meditation music and smelling delicate incense permeating the room. She had recently decided to enroll in an extensive Reiki certification program. The system had always interested her, but for one reason or another, she never found the right opportunity to try it out until now.

"Okay. Take a last deep breath, and open your eyes." The hotel event room was rather small, but adequate for the ten participants, including the instructor. "So, why don't we go around the circle and present ourselves?" he said, starting with an older woman who had brought along her twenty-something son. One after the other, the partakers commented about who they were and what they did, and Aline quickly picked up on the tendency of the group: homeopaths, caregivers, healers, and Reiki practitioners.

"Hello, everyone. My name is Aline Belanger, Regional Director of Security for the Company, and I'm here to open up my horizons to energy work." Silence. The surprised faces and expressions of, "Are you sure you're in the right place?" really amused her, so much so that she couldn't stifle her snicker.

Before she could continue, the twenty-something guy googled the Company and read the information aloud. "Biggest gold-mining corporation in Mexico, with operations in Guerrero, Chihuahua, and Zacatecas. Wow. Pretty risky, huh?"

"Yes, as a matter of fact. Very risky," she said.

"Well, I am sure that the first Reiki symbol will help you out there," interjected the mother confidently. Aline gave her a polite smile, at that moment not knowing that in the future, before every flight to and from the mines and for any dodgy situation that merited it, she would very subtly trace the first symbol of protection to help ensure that everything went as smoothly as possible.

"And where are you from?" asked a blonde-haired woman a little further along the circle.

"Canadá."

"Oh. Me imagino con un frío espantoso, no?"

"A veces," Aline replied.

For the next three days, they improved their meditation skills and discussed theoretical information and the application of the four Reiki symbols, with hours of hands-on techniques to perfect form.

"Muy bien, Aline," commented the instructor after she had repeated a sequence of movements that he had demonstrated only moments before. "Have you had any type of training prior to this gathering?"

"Well, years of martial arts, mostly external, although in some of the systems we did focus on internal chi kung techniques, meditation, and auto-suggestion," she replied.

"Ah. That would explain it."

At the end of the program, the rank of shihan was conferred upon her under the Japanese system of Gendai Reiki Ho.[34]

****

It was a hot and humid day in mid-April. Aline and her security team were in Cocoyoc, Morelos on a two-day team-building workshop. The locale was a sixteenth-century colonial *hacienda*, with lots of open spaces, grass, trees, and a functional aqueduct. It was actually very serene and a nice place to reflect on things. She

34 Gendai Reiki Ho—The modern Reiki method of healing. "Ho" means method or technique, and "Gendai" signifies modern. The fourth level is Gokuikaiden, rank of shihan (i.e., master), imparted by A. Würth, from the training lineage of Mikao Usui, Kanichi Taketomi, Kimiko Koyama, Hiroshi Doi, and A. Würth.

liked the accommodations, particularly the spacious, sunken, ceramic-tiled shower that was constructed in such a way that a set of stairs from the main floor led downward directly into it. The back patio outside had an in-ground, private, miniature pool, which was actually closer to the size of a large bathtub more than anything else. One could only wade in about neck-deep.

"Hmm. Worth taking a closer look a little later on," Aline said.

That evening, after a series of long work sessions, the group had dinner and then turned in for the night. The sun had already set as she walked to her bungalow, and the moon was rising. Everything was dark and quiet. The air was fresh, bordering on cool. Placing the key into the door lock, she entered and went to the bathroom for a towel. She removed her clothes and opened the sliding door, which led to the back. Crossing the short patio, she dropped her towel and entered the pool. Making little to no sound, she submerged herself in the water. Cold. Much colder than she expected. After five minutes, she waded toward the edge. "That should pretty much do it," she mused. "Time for a hot shower." She raised her body up and out of the pool and covered herself with the towel. Returning inside, she headed straight for the steps of the shower.

****

Her phone vibrated. Aline reached for her cell on the night table. She already had on her warm PJs and was ready for bed. It was a WhatsApp text message from Selene:

—¿ Que onda, ca?

—Nada. Descansando.

—What are you doing this weekend? We have an awesome fiesta planned. A band is flying in from up north. Can you come?

Aline thought for a moment. *Banda music? Ni modo.*

—Claro. Nos vemos allí.

—*Órale*. Beso.

Saturday night at a private hacienda in Guerrero. Armed "guards" in cowboy hats stood at the gates with earpieces, checking names, cars, and personal belongings.

"Buenas noches, señorita. Please step out of the vehicle. ¿Su nombre?"

"Aline Belanger. Soy amiga de Selene."

After they confirmed her name on the guest list and double-checked it via portable radio, Aline got back into her car and drove up to the main house. Selene was waiting for her on the steps to the front door, garbed in a sheer, white, low-cut dress with open-toed heels.

"Hola, amiga."

"Hola," Aline responded as they exchanged customary alternating kisses on the cheek. The valet drove away with her car as they entered the house. The stately foyer had marble floors and alcoves housing statues of semi-nude Greek deities, a cathedral ceiling with a chandelier, and walls adorned with French Impressionist paintings.

"Looks like Monet," said Aline.

"Así es," answered Selene.

"¿Champaña, señoritas?" asked a waiter, holding out a tray with glasses filled with Louis Roederer Cristal.

"Sí, joven. Gracias. Salud, amiga."

"Salud," replied Aline, tilting her head backwards to sip the bubbly while taking note of the guard at the top of the stairs, brandishing his *cuerno de chivo*.[35]

"Vamos al baño," insisted Selene, latching on to Aline's arm and pulling her down the corridor. At the end of the hallway on the right was a large bathroom that was pleasing to the eye, with subtly mixed tones of blue and turquoise on the tiles and ceramic finishes. Selene closed the door, locking it slowly behind them, and then turning, produced a small, cylindrical glass vial from out of nowhere. Aline was astonished. Selene had no purse on her, and undeniably, no bra or panties under her dress. Selene giggled and pulled Aline closer to her and then down to one of the low, plush, velvet divans and emptied the contents of the receptacle onto an accompanying table. White powder, although Aline noticed a very distinct hint of bright yellow in the mixture.

"¿Qué es?" she asked.

"Coca nena con oro puro," she said impishly while skillfully cutting the substance into fine lines using paraphernalia readily available on the tabletop.

"¿Estás loca, Selene?"

"Ha. It's better than inhaling it with gunpowder," she replied, snorting an ample dose. "Te toca, cabrona."

35 *Cuerno de chivo*—Slang term used exclusively in Mexico to refer to the AK-47 assault rifle, also known as a Kalashnikov.

Puta madre, Aline thought, leaning over. She plugged her right nostril while pulling air in hard with the left. *Chasing white rabbits down holes; go ask Aline when she's ten feet tall.*[36]

As they walked toward the back of the house, Aline could hear the live *banda* music getting louder and louder.

It's not that bad when you think about it, Aline thought. *Or maybe it is just the drugs talking.* When they got to the tent, Aline was taken aback by the magnitude of the party—hundreds upon hundreds of people eating, drinking, and dancing; armed men positioned every few meters; others patrolling with dogs; service staff attending guests; and enough bling-bling to merit a casting for a hip-hop video.

They made their way to Teniente's table.

"Buenas noches, Aline. ¿Cómo has estado?"

"Muy bien, gracias."

The ladies sat down, and a waiter serving exclusive tequila and mezcal stock immediately attended them.

"Here's to new friends," toasted Teniente. "Salud." They all downed their *caballitos* in one shot, which were instantaneously replaced by another.

At about midnight, Aline noted the arrival of a short, moustached man with a notable gut wearing a flamboyantly patterned, blue, long-sleeved shirt with chains and jewelry, a big belt buckle, and a .45 caliber, gold-plated pistol tucked behind it. He was escorted

36 Reference to Lewis Carroll's Alice in Wonderland. A lyrical interpretation of the song "White Rabbit," Jefferson Airplane's 1967 psychedelic anthem.

by a couple of ladies on his arms and five *sicarios*, who could have tried out for the offensive line of any NFL franchise.[37]

"Who's that?" Aline asked, sitting up in her chair.

"That is El Líder, my boss," said Teniente.

The Leader made his way through the crowd, everyone making a noticeable and concerted effort to smile and greet him. The women gave respectful kisses on the cheek. The men, using the standard greeting among friends, shook hands with him, gave a formal hug with two firm, successive back slaps, and then gave another handshake. As El Líder reached their table, Aline could almost swear that she smelled testosterone in the air mixed with expensive, musky cologne.

"Compadre. ¿Qué me cuentas?" he directed toward Teniente.

"Pues, nada. Aquí estamos, compadre."

El Líder shifted his eyes to Aline as he moved closer and took her right hand in his. "And you must be la famosa Señorita Aline," he said, bringing up her hand to his mouth and kissing it gallantly. "I have heard many good things about you."

"Encantada, señor. Aline Belanger, a sus *órdenes*."

"Ay Chihuahua. Your Spanish is very good, señorita," he said delightedly.

"Muchas gracias."

They took their seats and picked up where they had left off with the drinking, this time including the guest of honor. The band continued and eventually took a break, replaced temporarily by a deejay who

37 NFL—National Football League.

started to play Vicente Fernandez ballads from a very sophisticated sound system.

"May I have this dance?" asked Teniente, extending his hand toward Aline.

"Claro que sí."

"So, how are you getting along with Selene?"

"Fine. She's fun," answered Aline.

"Yes, she is, isn't she?" he asked rhetorically. "You know, you look somewhat tired and perhaps a little stressed. Everything all right in the mining world?"

"Yes, of course. You know, there's always plenty to do when you're looking for gold," Aline said with a grin.

"I can imagine. Mira. A good amigo of mine has a very nice resort in Playa del Carmen. Let me give him a ring and arrange that you spend a few days there as my guest."

CHAPTER 7

Aline luxuriously stretched herself to the full extent of her body on the poolside bed, looking out over the ocean. Two years in the mining industry had blown by—protecting personnel, assets, and the Corporate image, managing perpetual crises, mitigating risk, and single-handedly creating a department from scratch that spearheaded initiatives and facilitated the work of other areas while the Company continued to focus myopically on a single directive: the production of gold. *Pinches mineros*, she thought.

She was back in Playa del Carmen (where else?) drinking *mojitos* and enjoying the shade and warm breeze. As her mind drifted, Aline thought about what she had seen in relation to criminal organizations—violence, brutality, and excessive, if not eccentric, lifestyles. But what never ceased to amaze her was the blatant, unabashed emotional disconnect demonstrated time and again. Whether coked-up or high on whatever narcotic they had in their possession, the grizzly acts being carried out were simply inhuman. And therein lay the present, paradoxical conundrum on the verge of insanity: a macho society with a predominantly, albeit latent, matriarchal foundation intertwined with deeply rooted sentiments toward family. How could someone morally justify the torture, mutilation, and execution of a person knowing that they are causing profound harm, not just to the victims but also to their families? Something they themselves would obviously want to avoid if they or someone from their own family were the target? Unadulterated disassociation or maybe just downright evil incarnate.

"Otro mojito, por favor," Aline gestured to the poolside waiter.

Aline would later capitalize on the role of the societal maternal figure, integrating it into the regional corporate security strategy. In discussions with her coworkers from community relations, she would tropicalize the concept of stakeholder engagement, concentrating specifically on the matriarchs of the communities near the Company's operations and how to involve them more directly with the mine. This would become manifest through requests for services of embroidering Company logos on shirts and jackets, food preparation for events, and the like. By doing so, not only was the Company creating micro-economies in the area, but it was also associating the ladies of the community with the Corporation, essentially creating ambassadors of the grandmothers, mothers, and aunts, who in some instances had familial relationships with the local narcos. This could translate into real and tangible examples of why their boys should leave the Company alone.

As the sun began to set, Aline gathered up her belongings, placed them into her beach bag, and headed back to the presidential suite. *Nice touch on Teniente's part,* she thought. The ostentatious penthouse had all the amenities that anyone could want: lush tropical foliage, blooming flowers, its own palm trees, indoor and outdoor hot tubs, and a rain shower on the terrace without walls or glass enclosures—just you, the water, and the open sea air.

The same afternoon that Aline had arrived at the resort, she found a large, sealed, foam-cushioned envelope with her name on the front next to the chocolate mints on the pillow. Opening it, she dumped the contents onto the bed: twenty-five thousand U.S. dollars in cash in crisp, one-hundred-dollar bills separated into neat bundles along with a handwritten note:

> Aline, disfruta tu estancia. I'm sure you will find the terrace shower relaxing. —Teniente

Placing the beach bag onto one of the chairs, she peeled off her clinging, wet bikini and walked unabashedly to the terrace, turning on the water of the rain shower to wash off the sweat, sand, and suntan lotion. The strong torrent cascaded over her supple frame as she lathered with bath gel and rinsed for a while, enjoying the experience, which left her skin taut and refreshed. Air-drying her body with the warm breeze, she looked out over the ocean and took in the salty air.

She went back inside, stepping into the spacious, mirrored walk-in closet and surveyed the additional extravagances that Teniente had prepared for her: a pristine, exquisite black evening dress, a chic ladies' gold wristwatch, necklace and earrings displayed on a dark velvet tray on one of the shelves, and a designer purse and shoes in her size immaculately placed below.

"Está chingón," she said aloud, referring to her welcome package.

She got dressed, did her hair and makeup, then opened the suite's safe box to pull out one of the bundles of cash. Opening the purse to store the money, she came across a tiny glass vial identical to Selene's. Aline unplugged the vessel and paused for a brief instant, as if waiting for the little voice inside of her head to shout and scream in protest that this was an outrage, some kind of mistake or misunderstanding, that they had dragged the wrong person into this reality and that at any moment her hand would rise and defiantly throw the miniature ampoule against the wall like the Archangel Michael armed with the sword from God's armory, besting Satan in personal combat. Shattering it into a thousand pieces, she would laugh triumphantly, drunk with victory over the annihilation of this daunting nemesis. Silence. Then the voice did speak to her in a clear and calm demeanor. "No. There is no error here. You are where you are by your own free will and being. No ominous hand is at play." Stillness. Looking into her eyes in the mirror, she stared for some time, then whispered, "So be it." With full resolve, she emptied a portion of the contents onto the back of her hand and inhaled the golden mixture sharply, marking the genesis of her downward spiral.

****

She was on a one-day trip to the city of Chihuahua to interview candidates for a security management position at the Chihuahua mine. As the regional security area was rapidly evolving into a highly sophisticated and effective organism, Aline needed to incorporate key all-star players at each level who could replicate the corporate mandate in their respective fields of influence.

She had programmed two separate interviews at a restaurant in the airport. The first candidate walked in and sat down lethargically, and Aline could see by his movements and manner of response that in a crisis situation he would be slow to react and inevitably suffer from a mental shutdown.

"Thank you very much. We will keep you informed regarding the progress of your application." She turned her attention to the server after the applicant left. "Joven. Un jugo verde y un popote, por favor."

"*Sí*, señorita."

While she slowly sipped her cold green juice—a mixture of orange, nopal, and celery—the second applicant burst into the restaurant, provoking mild anxiety in some of the patrons. Spotting Aline, he made a beeline for the table.

"Buenos días. ¿Señorita Aline?" he barked. This candidate was the extreme opposite of the first guy in a bad way. Black combat fatigues and boots, high-strung, and basically gung-ho about everything.

"Could you please describe your concept of security, the applied methodology that you use, and your overall strategy?" she asked.

"Yes. It all comes down to one simple solution: an assault rifle and a permit to carry."

Aline refrained from spitting out her juice and saying something like, "You've got some serious issues, buddy." Instead, she replaced it with a neutral response and muddled through the rest of the conversation.

"Okay then. I think that's all I need. Thank you for your time. We'll be in contact."

Aline put her documents into her portfolio and asked for the check. "I guess we have to keep looking for the right person," she said disappointedly.

****

"¿Otro tequila, señorita?" asked the waiter.

"Sí, por favor," Aline answered. *Un poco sacado de onda,* she thought. For a split second, she wasn't quite sure of where she was. "Oh yeah, Acapulco. At one of Teniente's five-star hotels on the Pacific Coast."

As night fell, the open patio bar was lit with gas torches. Live piano music played to a sparse crowd of about three persons at a distant table. After all, it was a Monday and not tourist season.

Teniente approached her in a white *guayabera* shirt, linen pants, and canvas shoes, with a page-sized envelope in his hand.

"Buenas noches, amiga. ¿Cómo te va?"

"Bien, gracias."

He sat and lit a cigarette, drawing the smoke in slowly and blowing it out even slower. "So, here we are," he said, looking at her closely. "You may recall when I told you that I needed someone like you in my organization." It was more of a statement than a question. "It's time you started making the amounts of money that I promised you." He opened the envelope and pulled out a high-resolution photograph of a forty-something guy, stocky, pudgy-faced, and light-skinned with curly hair. "Do you recognize this man?"

Aline looked over the man's features, studying his face and eyes, and unmistakably recognized him from a DEA report she had read. It was El Coyote, leader of a faction vying for dominance in El Líder's territory. She remembered that he had outstanding arrest warrants for his involvement in multiple homicides, kidnappings, and extortions in the United States as well as Mexico, and was pretty much wanted dead or alive.

"No, I don't know him," she said convincingly. "Who is he?"

"His name is El Coyote, and he is a very bad man," he said. (She grinned inside, thinking, *El burro hablando de orejas*). "I need you to take care of him," he said in a hushed tone.

Expressionless, Aline continued to look him in the eye. "When and where?"

"In about a month, he will be visiting his usual nighttime venue in Naucalpan in the State of Mexico. As his group has had sole control of this area for some time now, his security will actually be lower than anywhere else. I will give you instructions once I receive a confirmed date and place. Everything will be very quick."

Back in the regional office in Mexico City, Aline googled Naucalpan, familiarizing herself with the main streets, alternate routes, landmarks, and locations of various bars and police stations. Workwise, she had recently brought aboard a former professional colleague whom she had met a number of years back through common membership in a group made up of corporate security executives.

Lewis was a happy-go-lucky guy in his forties who had worked as head of security for a German automotive company with headquarters in Stuttgart and later worked in telecommunications. He was the *bonachón* of the office, someone you would send to become buddy-buddy with people from the other areas who were hostile toward the Security Department. He was responsible for Operational Support & Projects. Adding to the lineup was Frank, a seasoned professional and senior security manager from a pharmaceutical giant. He was the go-to guy for implementing an institutional security program, and he was the manager of Risk & Intelligence. Together, they would tackle the relentless workload and divvy up tasks accordingly, always upholding the practice of roundtable communication where all opinions and viewpoints were expressed openly and heard without fear of repercussion.

The achieved synergistic relationships and sophisticated outputs would become unparalleled in the Company, elevated to a level not often seen in an organization that was not funded by some government entity.

****

Friday evening at 8:45 p.m., Aline got a short text message from Teniente:

Bulbo. 11:00 p.m. Cuarto cubículo.

"Enterada," she texted back. Aline slipped out of her sweatpants and T-shirt and started to get ready for her assignment, adding a straight-haired, dark wig to her getup. By 9:25 p.m., she was out the door, requesting a taxi from an authorized site nearby.

"¿A dónde va, señorita?" asked the cabbie as she stepped into the vehicle and closed the door, setting the lock.

"El antro Bulbo en Naucalpan, por favor."

The drive took about twenty minutes or so, and there was already a considerable line along the side of the building. Even though ladies were usually fast-tracked into the club, particularly ones that were unaccompanied, Aline did not want to take any chances. She pulled out two folded five-hundred-peso bills from her evening purse and subtly showed them to the bouncer, who had a clipboard in hand and was talking into a headset. After a few minutes, he steered her in.

Loud. So much so that Aline could feel the beat of the electronic music pulsing through her entire body while darkness was juxtaposed with blinding strobe lights and programmed laser patterns. She could faintly make out fluorescent letters, indicating restrooms. Maneuvering around couples swept up in euphoric waves of passion, kissing and pressing their bodies together, she entered the door marked "*damas*." The fourth stall had a sign on it that read "*fuera de servicio.*" Placing her left shoulder against it, she shoved, and the door gave way easily. Entering, she latched it closed behind her. There was a window in the stall, partially open. Aline brought the toilet seat cover down and stood on it to get a closer look. It was small but manageable. Looking through the limited space between the actual window and its frame, she could see that it connected to a dark alleyway, which was no higher than two meters from the ground. Stepping back down, she opened the tank cover of the toilet and found a plastic bundle stuck to it with duct tape. She separated it and, replacing the cover, proceeded to open the package: a black, snub-nose .38 caliber revolver with concealed hammer. She examined the piece with precision—filed-off serial numbers and in good overall condition. Opening the cylinder with ease, she looked over the five rounds and pulled one out: hollow-point.[38] Returning the round to its original housing, she closed the cylinder and tucked the weapon into her purse.

Upon leaving the bathroom, she paused to soak up her surroundings. Looking right, she noticed a corridor that veered to the left, which was almost imperceptible from the main hallway. She took a few steps and followed the pathway as it swung left, ending in an entrance covered with two long pieces of transparent silk fabric. Separating the soft material, she entered quietly. She found herself in a small, private room, almost chamberlike. There was no one there. Plush chairs and couches, purple (or were they black?) in color. Aline couldn't determine which since the room was only lit with black light. This was unquestionably the VIP lounge used for private entertainment. She looked down at her glowing watch. It was 10:50 p.m. She exited the lounge and reintegrated into the ever-growing crowd without effort, finding a strategic viewpoint from which she could see—with eyes now a bit more adjusted to the darkness—the main entrance to the club and who walked toward the bathrooms.

....

38 Hollow-point—A bullet that expands upon entering a target. These bullets are utilized to decrease penetration and maximize tissue damage and blood loss.

At 11:15 p.m., El Coyote sauntered in. Medium height and thick-bodied, he was already sweating through his silk shirt. He had so much gold jewelry on that the laser lights actually reflected off of him, giving the appearance of an almost celestial being. "Now that's what I call irony in motion," she laughed. Three muscle-bound apes served as his personal security. They accompanied him to a sectioned-off area where an eager female host received and escorted him to a secluded table. A waiter stood by to take his order and shortly thereafter returned with a bottle of exclusive tequila.

Aline sipped her mineral water, staying calm and alert, all the while discreetly monitoring El Coyote as he shoveled food into his face and downed alcohol as if it were water. By 12:30 a.m., he was a bit wobbly. Only one of his security personnel remained close to him; the other two had withdrawn a while back, one staying around the main entrance, and the other somewhere out of sight. *He probably returned to the car to catch a few z's,* thought Aline.

El Coyote gestured to the host, who attentively approached and bent down toward him to receive some sort of instructions and then walked off. A couple of minutes later, El Coyote stood up from the table and was guided to the VIP lounge while his security guy planted himself casually near the entry point of the hallway leading to the restrooms.

"This is it," Aline said to herself. Standing, she subtly pulled her Lycra dress downward at the waist to reveal more of her cleavage and headed provocatively toward the tired and bored goon.

“Hola,” she said with a smile. “Me comentaron que tu jefe estaba esperándome.”

The goon leered at her and gazed down her front. “Adelante, señorita.”

Passing security, she took a deep breath and entered through the hanging sheer material once again. “Buenas noches, señor. Soy Samantha.”

“Buenas noches, Samantha,” said El Coyote, eyeing her fully from head to toe. “Eres muy guapa.”

“Muchas gracias.” Aline quickly noticed the pair of engraved .38 Supers at his disposal, one on the small, round table in front of him and the other, with hammer cocked, close at his side. *Shit. This could get ugly,* she thought.

“Señorita. Why don’t you come here and sit on my lap?” he asked, patting his knee, already noticeably excited. She smiled and nodded, taking a couple of steps toward him. “Would you like something special, para empezar?” she asked, already reaching into her purse with her left hand.

“Of course,” he answered. Pulling the revolver out, she let the purse drop and aimed center mass, while El Coyote, as if blessed with a sixth sense, simultaneously reached for the pistol by his thigh and fired off a hip shot, grazing Aline’s right shoulder as she discharged the five rounds into her target. Knowing that she only had a few seconds before his bodyguard arrived, she grabbed a champagne bottle by the neck from an ice bucket and positioned herself to the left side of the entrance close to the wall. The security guy burst in, pistol drawn, and was blindsided by the bottle, which came crashing down onto the base of his skull, dropping him to the ground. Stepping over the man's body, Aline made sure that El Coyote had no vital signs and then slipped off one of his thick, gold pinky rings. Picking up her purse, she stashed the gun and the ring and ran toward the ladies' room. When she reached the fourth stall, she kicked open the door and stepped up onto the seat. She braced her palm against the window frame and pushed forcefully, easily dislodging the weak hinges. Throwing the purse out first, she hoisted herself up and slid out through the opening, dropping down into the alley and escaping into dark shadows: Angelorum Lapsus beckoning.[39]

****

Monday morning, *café* in hand, Aline entered the corporate building and stepped into the elevator, pressing number fifteen.

"Buenos días, Aline," said the receptionist.

"Buenos días, Norberta."

Aline walked to her office and unlocked the door. "Hola muchachos. ¿Cómo les fue el fin?"

"Bien. ¿Y tú?"

"Bien. Todo tranquilo," she replied.

"What's with your shoulder?" asked Lewis, astutely observing that she was moving a bit slower than usual and doing things with her left hand that she normally did with her right.

"It's probably an old shoulder injury from a few years back, most likely from one of my fights, so this

39 Angelorum Lapsus—In Latin, this means "Fallen Angels."

morning I had an appointment to get a PRP injection from a specialist that I found a few blocks up on Avenida Palmas."[40]

"Oh. Sounds painful."

"Algo," she replied.

****

Arriving at Monterrey International Airport, a Company driver was already waiting for her. It was May. She was traveling to the new project, located about fifty kilometers east of the Zacatecas mine in San Tiburcio situated in the municipality of Mazapil, Zacatecas. Because the drive from the airport would be about three hours, she settled into her seat for a light snooze. At the time, the project had considerable potential, with a Company investment of USD $80 million destined for pre-feasibility studies. Unfortunately, the price of gold would eventually start to fall, and within the timespan of about a year and a half, plummet below the USD $1,200 per-ounce mark, driving the Company to suspend project operations indefinitely and begin implementation of its divestment strategy across the region.[41]

On the bright side, gold prices were presently strong, the Company continued to invest in projects, and Aline knew that this was the right moment to

....

40 PRP Injection—A therapy in which platelet-rich plasma (PRP) is derived from a patient's own blood and then injected into the wounded area to stimulate healing.

41 When Aline had joined the Company, the price of gold per ounce had surpassed USD $1,800.

start taking intelligence-driven security to the next level. She drew up a design for the model that she had envisioned for the Security Department, not only in Mexico but in all of the Americas respectively, from Canada to Argentina, including the Caribbean.

The concept was simple: intelligence over IQ. However, Aline had found there was a scarcity of both throughout the organization. Intel, the useful information concerning a subject of interest, was most important. Aline was exceedingly cautious in using the term "intelligence" since it quickly connoted government agencies à la the CIA, NSA, or the former KGB—secret agendas, cloak-and-dagger intrigue, or successful box-office hits with amnesic protagonists in search of their identities and retribution against the organization that put them there in the first place. She opted to replace the word "intel" with "information."

"Let's see," imagined Aline, sitting with her fingers interlocked behind her head, looking around her office and thinking of the space where this information gathering and analysis would take place. "A room relatively soundproof with tinted glass, or at least some type of opaque film, applied to its surface to impede curious coworkers from seeing who or what was going on inside. Biometric access control. No iris scanning required, though; fingerprint identification will suffice. A skilled knowledge officer with the right profile, of course, who will be tasked with specific duties and assignments. And the pièce de résistance, kick-ass intelligence software."

After a number of brainstorming sessions to come up with an appropriate and functional name, the area in question would come to be officially known as the IGC—the Information Gathering Center—*the* intelligence initiative that would propel Mexico's Regional Security Department to the forefront of all of the Company's mining operations in the Americas.[42]

The next step was the software itself. Coincidentally, as they began to discreetly search for potential products, an established corporation approached them with an intelligent solution that was anything but. With great enthusiasm, the corporation's president of Scandinavian descent presented a mobile tactical vehicle with collapsible antenna and ground-anchoring mechanisms for support. "All you have to do is station the vehicle in the area of your mine operations, enable the system, and you're ready to monitor communication, track objectives, and process information."

This is just a bad scenario from every angle, no matter how you look at it, Aline thought. She took a deep breath before answering, trying to calm the knee-jerk response of rebuking the executive and the group that came with him for completely and unequivocally failing to understand the needs of a potential business client. "The areas where the Company operates are very remote. All movements are monitored by Organized Crime, and in some cases, by federal agencies," she continued. "Installing a vehicle of this type would draw serious attention from both the good guys and the bad guys. If the crime groups got wind of such equipment, they would surely commandeer it and the

....

42 In Spanish, the IGC is CGI, or the *Centro de Gestión de Información.*

corresponding operators, most likely assuming that it was some sort of operation conducted by a government agency. And if the agencies detect the vehicle, we can expect that they would also act on the assumption that this could be a counterintelligence effort from well-funded Organized Crime, confiscate the equipment, take the operators into custody for questioning, and later lay charges against the Company for the violation of a number of Privacy of Information Acts."

The group was dumbfounded, and the president was at a loss for words.

Continuing with the search, they came across an Israeli-based corporation offering a software that could be administered in-house and that was more in line with what Aline needed—the monitoring of open-source information, such as news and media reports; the capacity to create taxonomies of persons, groups, and social networks; extrapolate trends and tendencies; and on occasion, fashion an avatar or two that could partake in group chats that often consisted of extremist and radical anti-mining organizations intent on destroying Company property or carrying out violent acts.[43]

After a series of meetings, demonstrations, and telephone conferences with Tel Aviv, Aline was convinced that she had identified the product that she wanted. The security team would immediately start a closed tendering process of at least three contenders for the contract. As the software was not that readily available, there were a limited number of corporations

43 Avatar–Online personification or representation.

in Mexico that could provide licensing rights, required hardware, support, and options for future upgrades. By process of elimination, the corporation based in Israel with an in-country office was the first choice in terms of complying with all of the requirements. It would eventually win the contract.

Meanwhile, Aline started the required CAPEX budgeting for the acquisition of the software,[44] simultaneously putting into effect her strategy of stakeholder mapping and engagement. The Company was quite adept at identifying its stakeholders, or interest groups; however, it was grossly unskilled at implementing an effective plan of engagement. She made sure not to perpetuate that error.

"So, who do think will be our primary internal backer for the IGC?" asked Frank.

"Well, considering that we're talking about software and everything that goes with it, hands down I'd place my bet on the vice president of Information Technology from the Vancouver office, who happens to be really pro on security."

"Oh, hey Aline," said the VP of IT. "How are things in Mexico?"

"Just fine, thanks. Do you have a minute?"

"Sure. What's on your mind?"

"We're moving a really great security initiative that will benefit all Company operations, and I wanted to get your input on it."

"Sounds interesting. What is it?"

....

44 CAPEX–Capital expenditure. Software programs are considered intangible, fixed assets whenever the owning entity (i.e., the Company) controls those assets through custody or legal rights.

"Well, in essence, it's intelligence-gathering software."

"Ooh, now you've got my attention," he laughed.

"I thought it would," she responded, laughing as well. "It's an Israeli software, considered 'smart' since it learns to autonomously adjust search parameters according to what the user needs."

"And who has used this software? Mossad?" he joked.

"Maybe. But what really interests us is the fact that with very little training, we can kick-start the system and start processing intel from day one. So, what I need from you is support with respect to keeping in line with Company IT policies, hardware requirements, backup servers off-site, and maintenance."

"Okay. That part is easy. Here comes the million-dollar question. How much is this puppy gonna cost?"

"It's funny that you express it that way. The software is actually close to a million bucks."

"Whoa," uttered the VP. "Is that the final price?"

"Not even close," she said. "You know how it is when people hear that the Company is looking to acquire something. They get a spark in their eye thinking about gold bars and positive cash flow, and that undoubtedly influences what they want to charge us. I'm pretty sure that if we move ahead with the project and show them we are serious, they will be more than willing to adjust the amount."

The next phase of Aline's plan was organizing a tasty breakfast meeting in the boardroom where she would present the scope of the concept. She reasoned that it was always good to have executives avoid making decisions on an empty stomach.

“And as I mentioned from the beginning of the presentation, the first phase will be to run a pilot test in real time before making any significant financial commitments,” Aline said, looking directly at the CFO. “Moreover, if you are generally in agreement with this project, then I will be approaching each of you for a one-on-one follow-up meeting to explain the minutiae of the undertaking and the tangible benefits that your area will receive from this software. And wouldn’t it be great,” she continued, “if you knew who you were going into a meeting with when approaching ejido leaders and their legal defense?” asked Aline of the director of the Legal Department.

“It does sound intriguing,” she replied, puffing out a soft stream of vapor from her e-cigarette.

“And the system can be set up to automatically run very specific search profiles day and night concerning attorneys, lawsuits, and organizational affiliations, just to name a few.”[45]

****

“Looks like your stakeholder engagement plan turned out to be right on the button,” said Lewis, chomping down on a baguette at Le Pain Quotidien on Avenida Palmas, close to the office.

45 On a future occasion, Aline provided the director with background information concerning a lawyer in the state of Zacatecas who was intentionally misleading communities in an attempt to undermine the Company. In reality, he was pushing personal interests that involved his wife, who intended to build a hospital and appoint herself general director and place family members on staff. The information provided by the system was used effectively as leverage to discredit the lawyer.

"Yeah," Aline replied, sipping her cappuccino from a bowl-like mug with no handle. "The only real naysayer, though, was Woody." Woody was the director of Corporate Affairs who happened to report directly to the egocentric, somewhat-lacking-in-political-savvy SVP who had now ascended to EVP in Vancouver. "He summed up the software as being nothing more than a sophisticated Google search."

"Hmm. That's a bit odd, don't you think?" asked Lewis. "He's usually very pro-security, and he definitely respects you."

"Maybe, although I think that it may have to do with the fact that the software and the IGC itself represent a potential threat to the EVP's hefty contract with the consulting firm working out of Washington, D.C. Imagine for a minute that our intelligence initiative is successful, providing useful data and analysis to all of the regions. That could very quickly bring up questioning from the EVP's boss—the president & CEO—as to why the Company continues to dish out an exorbitant amount of money for intel to the American consultants if we can do it all in-house."

"You could be right. I never thought about it that way."

With the IGC infrastructure completed and the purchase of the software and hardware underway, Aline started the process of hiring a knowledge officer, interviewing a small handful of possible candidates.

"How's the search for the KO going?" asked Frank.

"Okay, I guess. I'm just not convinced by the individuals I've talked to so far."

"Well, this morning I received a resume from a trusted professional contact, and I think that she might be just right for the job."

"Great. Bring her in for an interview."

Claudette was a single mom in her early thirties, pleasant in nature, introverted, and rather shy, but definitely discreet. Experienced in information handling and data analysis, she fit the profile to a T. Right from the get-go, she started to tinker with the software, setting up Boolean searches and opening files on anti-mining groups. Her first task was to gather vast, real-time information—from Canada to Argentina—which would be synthesized and inserted into different types of reports depending on the context of the document. Whether CIDs (Comprehensive Information Digests) or the soon-to-be famous SUAs (Security Update Americas), intel was pouring into the IGC from everywhere.

"Here goes nothing," said the new knowledge officer a bit nervously, clicking on the "send" button to emit the first official SUA report of its kind:

[COMPANY LOGO]

Information Gathering Center
Mexico
IGC-SUA-001-****

Security Update Americas

Canada and USA

Canada General Overview: On ******, the ********* ******** ******** will hold a meeting in Montreal, with a session for the Canadian Mining Industry, where they plan to examine the role of Canadian mining companies in the violation of human and environmental rights in the region. The organizers are stating that there are over two hundred social conflicts relating to mining in Latin America and that 90% of these are linked to Canadian mining companies.

Ontario: No relevant information.
Quebec: No relevant information.
British Columbia: No relevant information.

USA General Overview: No relevant information.

South Dakota: No relevant information.
Reno: No relevant information.

Mexico

Chihuahua: Federal Forces arrested **** ****** ***** *****, head of the criminal cell "***** *****" of the ******* Cartel. This group has sustained confrontations with the ****** Cartel over control of the state.

Zacatecas: The anti-mining group ********** ** continues promoting its campaign "******** ***** ** ****" in addition to using the resolution of the agrarian court in Zacatecas that ordered the return of 600 ha of community land to the *Ejido* ***** ***** in Zacatecas.
Guerrero: Due to concerted government efforts against the criminal group *** ***** and its consequent restructuring, nine people were killed in the area of

Chilpancingo, and fifteen cab drivers were kidnapped (allegedly, the cab drivers were informants for *** *****).

Yesterday, ******, four people were killed in the community of Carrizalillo during a confrontation between the rival criminal groups *** ***** and ********* ******. In an official statement, authorities said that these violent acts are a result of the dispute over control in the area, instigated by the execution of a crime boss known as "El Coyote" last month in a nightclub located in Naucalpan, State of Mexico.

Mexico City: *** **** ****** has demonstrated significant infiltration within the ****** neighborhood in the center of Mexico City that to date was controlled by the ****** ** ** ***** ** ******, but because of security operations in Michoacán, this group lost terrain due to the complications of introducing drugs into Mexico City. *** **** ****** took advantage of these conditions and now controls the most important drug-selling points in ******.

Central and South America, Caribbean

General Overview Guatemala: The UN Commissioner in Guatemala urged the government to establish dialogue with the communities that are considered to be affected by mining activities, this as a reaction to the violent eviction of people in ** **** in a project of ********, subsidiary of ******, ********, and **********.

General Overview Chile: ******* **** reached an initial agreement with ******** communities in order to start with the ******-**** project; however, the communities and organizations contrary to the project are organizing a protest on ******.

General Overview Argentina: No relevant information.

General Overview Dominican Republic: No relevant information.

- END OF REPORT -

****

It was almost summer in Guerrero, if you could call it that; it was pretty much hot and humid all the time, with temperatures mid-year soaring to the point where you could actually cook an egg on the hood of a pickup. Aline made it a point to sit down with Joe L. from her team to talk about the security situation in the area.

"Well, it's surprising that one of the main crime bosses in the area, El Coyote, has apparently moved on," he exclaimed.

"Oh, that's odd," said Aline. *Not really,* she thought, given her little job in Naucalpan. *What is odd is the fact that the superintendent is obviously not reading the SUA reports emitted by the regional security office.* "Well, one thug less to deal with, I suppose."

"Yes. Unfortunately, there are still many to go around," added the superintendent.

That evening, Aline set out toward Chilpancingo, driving one of the mine's newly acquired (and undersized) two-door pickup trucks with the Company logo on the sides. She told Joe that she was having a dinner meeting with some officials in the city and would spend the night there. Approaching the outskirts of Chilpancingo, she was stopped at a search and seizure checkpoint, called *un retén*, with heavily armed "military" guys in fatigues who were obligating vehicles to pull over. One of them, using a handheld flashlight, directed her to the side of the road.

"Buenas noches, señorita. ¿De dónde viene?"

"Buenas noches. De la mina."

"Could I see some identification, please?"

"Yes, of course sir. Here you go," she said, handing him her Company ID. She noticed that his five o'clock shadow was well beyond that hour and his hair a bit too long for military standards. *Bogus checkpoint,* she supposed.

"Aline Belanger, correct?"

"Yes, that's right."

"And what do you do in the mine, señorita?"

"Maintenance."

"Ah," he said, not sounding too thrilled. "I believe that you are not Mexican. Is that right?"

"Yes, that's correct. I come from Canada."

"¿Canadá? ¿Es muy frío, no?"

"*Sí*. Muy frío," she replied, rolling her eyes slightly. During the chitchat, Aline observed that the guy had passed her ID to one of his colleagues, who had turned his back on them to make a cell phone call. A couple of minutes later, he walked toward them, ending the conversation with, "*Sí*, *sí*, está bien." He handed the ID back to his mate, who passed it along to her.

"Muchas gracias, señorita. Everything seems to be in order. Buenas noches."

"Gracias. Buenas noches." She drove off slowly, and about ten minutes later, she was on the boulevard where La Katrina was located. She pulled onto a nearby side street and parked the pickup. She wouldn't want anyone from the mine questioning why there was a Company vehicle right in front of a local bar.

The staff identified Aline as she walked in, and a friendly waitress that she also recognized greeted her. "Hola, chica. ¿Cómo estás? ¿Te sirvo un mojito?"

"Hola. Mejor una cerveza, por favor." One of the brutes she had clocked in the bathroom that first night was once again sitting at the bar. When he saw her, he gave her a nod, and she nodded back. Teniente was at his usual table, enjoying an order of *chalupas* and a cold Dos Equis lager.

"¿Cómo estás? Siéntate, por favor."

Taking a seat, she relaxed into her chair with a sigh. "Qué bueno qué es viernes."

"Tough day at the mine?"

"Something like that." The beer was cold, and she knocked back half of the bottle in one gulp. "You might as well bring me another and some chalupas, too," she said to the waitress.

Reaching into her pocket, Aline produced El Coyote's gold pinky ring and set it down softly close to Teniente's hand. He picked it up casually and, without looking at it, slipped it into his jeans.

"Muy bien, señorita. No esperaba menos de ti." She gave him a wry smile and finished off the first beer. "This is for you," he said, handing her a soft leather satchel. The bag was full and unusually heavy as she slung it over the back of the chair.

"Gracias."

"I will have a job for you coming up that I am sure you will find most interesting."

"Okay."

Three or four rounds later—she couldn't remember exactly how many—Aline got up and crossed the bag over her shoulder. "Ya me voy. Hasta luego."

"Hasta pronto," said Teniente.

Arriving at the same hotel that she had stayed at before, she pulled her overnight bag out of the pickup and made her way to the front desk.

"Buenas noches, Señorita Aline. Welcome back. We have been expecting you."

"Muchas gracias. Qué amable."

The receptionist handed her a key card, and Aline smiled. "Gracias. Buenas noches," she said as she walked toward the elevators. The room was quite ample but still had a cozy feel to it. Unlacing her safety boots, she kicked them off toward a corner and threw the satchel onto the king-size bed. She took off her polo shirt, unfastened her belt, removed her dusty jeans, and went to the bathroom to freshen up. Feeling a bit cleaner, she sat on the bed and reached for the remote. She flipped through the channels, stopping on the '90s flick, *Donnie Brasco*.[46]

"Let's see what's on the menu," she said, perusing the in-room card. Picking up the phone, she dialed t he restaurant.

"Buenas noches, Señorita Belanger. How may we be of service?"

....

46 *Donnie Brasco*—1997 American crime drama film starring Al Pacino and Johnny Depp.

"Hola. Un servicio a la habitación, por favor."

"Claro que *sí*."

"Sería un consomé de pollo y una limonada con agua mineral, por favor."

Hanging up, she pulled the leather bag over and undid the straps, emptying the contents. There was a shitload of cash—USD $100K to be exact—and a Colt .38 Super, model El Caballo de Oro Maximo, with an extra magazine. Admiring the gold engravings and designs in detail, she pressed the magazine release with her left index finger, pulling the magazine out with her right. Full. Replacing the magazine, she looked down the sights. "Bonita," she said, stowing everything away again. *Welcome to the ranks of the Fallen.*

Early the next week, Aline was at her desk, answering a slew of backlogged e-mails, when Roger, the security risk manager, walked into her office, closing the door behind him. Roger had filled a newly created position and reported directly to Mr. Straddler. Though he did not report to Aline, he felt that he could rely on and trust her with respect to Company matters, especially in Mexico. The tall, heavyset guy with glasses was pale and perspiring, even though the air-conditioning was on.

"¿Que pasó?" she asked.

"Yesterday I was invited for a late lunch by the new director of Community Relations to a nearby seafood place in Prado Norte, where we met with a couple of official-looking individuals. After our orders were taken and the waiter left, the director started talking openly with the gentlemen about problems that the Company was having with the ejidos in Zacatecas and the present and real risk of the mine being closed. 'La situación está cabrona,' emphasized the director. He was a tall and intense guy, and also fast-talking and thinking on his feet. He said, 'As we discussed, my colleague here,' referring to me, 'could meet with the person that you have recommended, perhaps someplace like Acapulco, and carry out the respective payment. Done deal.'"

"What?" asked Aline in disbelief. "They want to use you as a mule to deliver payment in cash?"

"*Sí*," he confirmed.

"That's just mental from every way you look at it. How would this play out? You driving to Acapulco carrying a briefcase full of money to a meeting? And if you were stopped by police, the military, or Organized Crime, couldn't you be mistaken for a narco? The lesser evil of the two would be the police arresting you, confiscating the money, and taking you into custody to await a lengthy sentence as a drug dealer, and if the criminals got ahold of you, you would most likely find yourself buried somewhere in Guerrero. This is just not going to happen," she affirmed.

"So what are we going to do?" asked Roger, now slightly relieved that he had gotten this new development off his chest.

"First, the fact that you approached me with the situation gets you off the hook by default because no one can question why you didn't share this information with Company management. Second, we will approach the director of Community Relations together and say that we discussed his plan, weighing the pros and cons, and that I considered it far too risky for you and the reputation of the Company, thereby stopping this issue dead in its tracks while you can save face. ¿Te late?"

"Sí. Muchísimas gracias, Aline."

"De nada."

****

A two-day trip to the Zacatecas mine in late August. As part of a regionwide security awareness campaign, Aline—in conjunction with Frank—had organized the well-known speaker and author, David Lee, to present his security manual on-site, complete with practical recommendations for work and everyday life.

"Nice turnout, don't you think?" said Aline to the site HR person who had helped organize the event.

"Yes. It's really incredible."

Over the two-day period, more than fifteen hundred employees participated in the presentations, which was a great success in terms of reaching the masses at the mine. Each person received their own copy of the little blue manual, extensively recognized and circulated in the security community. Aline had arranged for the purchase of the manuals in advance in order to ensure that each employee would get something tangible from the campaign that they could take home with them and share with their families. "Little details always go a long way," she said to herself.

Taking advantage of the visit to the mine, she wanted to follow up on a report that was recently emitted concerning the disappearance of a laboratory sample of Au worth about USD $1,500. The SOP for the confidential area in terms of handling samples was that after each test was completed, the sample would be returned to the safe, and two lab technicians were obliged to sign off on its safeguarding. On this occasion, one of the techs had apparently omitted this practice since the sample was unaccounted for the following morning. Because a limited number of persons had access to the laboratories, Aline had planned on interviewing each individual and then drawing up a timeline in order to identify any anomaly in the process, however insignificant. Unfortunately, the overeagerness of the director of Finance, who had previously worked on-site, shot the investigation to hell when he took it upon himself to inquire about the incident at lunchtime in one of the open mess halls.

"Does anyone have any information concerning the missing piece of gold from the laboratory last week?" he asked loudly, sitting at a crowded table.

****

As the month of October wrapped up, another incident catapulted the Regional Crisis Management Team into action. Kidnapping. Human Resources manager. The executive from the Zacatecas mine had been staying overnight at a hotel in Monterrey, when he apparently received a late-night call in his room from an unknown person claiming to be part of a powerful drug cartel that was looking for rival group members in the hotel.

"Quédate en tu cuarto, cabrón," said the voice on the phone in a threatening manner. "If you leave or call anyone, be assured that we are watching you and your family very closely, and if you fail to obey my instructions, you will pay the consequences."

This information was later relayed to Aline by a colleague of the HR manager, who was also staying at the hotel. During the time that the manager was receiving the call, he had apparently walked to his colleague's room to inform him of what was happening.

For the next two days and nine hours, Aline and her team backtracked over the existing information. They created a timeline of the event from the start to present day per Company protocol and established contact with local authorities, hotel staff, and the victim's family in order to maintain adequate and open communication channels. The manager's wife had informed them that during a brief telephone conversation with him, her husband utilized their predetermined, confidential phrase that was to be used only in case of an actual emergency or crisis.

"It just doesn't make sense," said Aline to Frank. "There were no police at the hotel on the night in question, and there was nothing out of the ordinary going on."

"That's right," responded Frank, flipping through his notes. "The only thing that the desk clerk said was that he noticed the manager on his cell phone and that he walked out of the lobby and into the street around 1:00 a.m."

"What about the hotel manager?"

"He only commented that there were no other reports from anyone else that night."

"Why would the Company HR manager have used the pre-established security phrase with his wife if there wasn't actually something wrong?" she asked.

"Don't know," said Frank.

****

Her cell phone vibrated. It was a call from Mr. Johnnie.

"Aline, are you near the corporate building? We have a crisis management call in progress in my office, and I think you should be in on it."

"I'm in the underground parking lot. I'll be up in three minutes."

Aline marched purposefully to the HR director's office and knocked on the plate-glass door, walking in. The MGM from the Zacatecas mine was on the line on loudspeaker. "Yes, I am sure. We have one of the kidnappers on another call talking with a manager. He's requesting a good-faith payment to expedite the release of the HR manager," he said nervously.

The conversation escalated to the point where everyone was talking all at once, causing tensions to rise. Aline bluntly interjected, addressing the MGM. "Listen. Tell him to hang up the damn phone," she commanded. There was a momentary hush as they assimilated what she had just ordered.

Then the MGM answered, "Okay."

"Also," she added, "tell your managers to turn off their cell phones. No one is to communicate with anyone." That little conversation between the manager and the kidnapper had already added another two hundred fifty thousand pesos to the pot, unfortunately.

Hanging up the call, Mr. Johnnie looked at Aline intensely through his glasses and said, "It is what it is," which was one of his two characteristic catchphrases, one that would become embedded in Aline's mind and always remind her of him in the future.[47]

....

47 The other phrase was "fuck," prolonging the "u" sound every time shit hit the fan or a crisis situation popped up, which was unfortunately very often.

The drama came to an end with the release of the HR manager, who was none the worse for wear, at least physically, considering that the entire escapade had been virtual.

"What?" asked Mr. Straddler on his cell phone, almost falling out of his chair.

"Yup," said Aline. "There was never any physical threat or adversary throughout the duration of the kidnapping. Yes, there was an actual call received, most likely from a prison or correctional facility." This was generally the method of choice for carrying out telephone extortions. "However, there was no real danger whatsoever."

"But I still don't understand. How did this ordeal last for more than two bloody days?" he insisted.

"Well, it was all a by-product of the temporary psychosis suffered by the HR manager. For a little less than sixty hours, he systematically, although unintentionally, maintained a live scenario wherein he moved from hotel to hotel—three to be precise—per received instructions, in addition to physically withdrawing money from various banks. In the debriefing, he told us that he had disguised himself with a baseball cap and change of shirt so as not to arouse suspicion."

"Suspicion from whom? The bank tellers?"

"No idea."

"And what about the phrase that he used when he contacted his wife?"

"Yeah, that," said Aline. "He did use the correct words to signal that there was an emergency. It's just that he utilized them to describe a situation that he himself was sustaining as a perceived danger."

"So, let me get this straight. No one at any point had this guy locked in a room somewhere or pointed a gun at his head?"

"That's correct. This was, in its entirety, a case of extortion."

"And the final damage incurred in terms of payout?"

"Combined with the multiple withdrawals from the banks and the contribution from the HR manager's colleague at the mine, the extortionists made off with a grand total of six hundred thousand pesos. Not bad for less than three days' work."

"That's brutal," he said.

"You know, there is a cherry on top to this incident," said Aline.

"Oh no. Let me have it."

"The fact is that the HR manager had recently participated in the security awareness sessions specifically concerning telephone extortions and how to react when confronting this type of situation.[48]

"That's just dandy."

****

Valle de Bravo, located in the State of Mexico, was chilly in February, with average temperatures between 8°C and 10°C. The mornings were downright cold at around 2°C. Three days of succession-planning meetings were scheduled for the Regional Management Team. The natural setting was secluded, with lots of trees and

48 The general rule is to stay calm, listen, and hang up. In the event that a member of the family is a victim, their whereabouts should be verified in order to discard the call as an extortion attempt.

underbrush, but paired with poor cell phone coverage and no television or radio in the small, one-room bungalow cabins with rustic decor. Quiet. The only sound was the breeze rustling leaves, and here and there, the odd call of a bird.

"Feels like some sort of spiritual retreat," said Aline, walking slowly—and very cautiously—down the uneven dirt-and-stone path to the main lodge-like building. "So much for these new shoes," she thought, looking at the scuffs and scratches now clearly visible on the Italian leather. She noticed that there were no in-ground lights on the paths. *Could get really tricky after dark. Make sure to get back to the cabin before nightfall,* she reflected.

From the left, she heard footsteps coming closer.

"Hey, how are you?" she asked, spotting her colleague from the Operational Excellence Department coming down another path.

"Great, and you?"

"Would have been nice if Human Resources had taken the time to inform us of the terrain so we could have at least brought the proper footware."

"You think?" he said, laughing and looking down at his muddied black dress shoes. "How's security?"

"Oh, you know. Always somebody in the Company doing something, and if not, then there's organized crime to keep you busy."

"No doubt. Wouldn't want to be dealing with your issues," he said.

"And how's it going with the sustainability of excellence?"

"Not everything is excellent," he answered somewhat unhappily. "Too many cuts in terms of people as the price of gold continues to fall. I don't understand how we can maintain best-in-class practices when we are letting our best people go..." He trailed off, almost as if he were talking to himself.

"I think we just take it day by day and do what we can," she said, trying for consolation.

"Yeah, I guess so."

After a small supper, Aline hurried back to her cabin. The sun had set, and dusk was setting in. The door creaked softly as she entered and flipped on the light switch. Low wattage bulbs reminded her of past visits she had made to small Eastern European villages under the Communist regime where electricity was considered a resource limited to helping you avoid bumping into things at night instead of a true source of light.

"No reading then," she sighed. "Guess I'll take a relaxing shower." She undressed, folding her clothes neatly on the bed, and covered herself with a white towel, which seemed only a little larger than a handcloth. "Hope there's hot water," she said with fading optimism. She turned on the faucet and let the water run for a few minutes. Lukewarm. "Man, this is really starting to suck," she said, closing the valve. "Might as well turn in."

For a while, Aline had been putting together a strategy for working her way into other high-level meetings with the National Commission of Security.[49] Through a third-party consultant utilized by the

49 National Commission of Security—In Spanish, this is the Comisión Nacional de Seguridad, or CNS.

Company, they were granted a meeting with the Office of the Commissioner to discuss security matters and establish contact with the current regional heads of Federal Police, particularly in the states of Guerrero, Zacatecas, and Chihuahua, the latter being responsible for Sinaloa and Sonora.

"Of course," said the female attaché of the commissioner, a dark-haired lady in her fifties with a strong personality that commanded respect. "We can set up individual meetings with the regional heads through our office as soon as possible. When would you be available to fly out and meet them?"

"Immediately," answered Aline.

"Thank you so much. That would be most helpful."

****

Bienvenidos a Miami, thought Aline. *Well, actually Hollywood, Florida, but close enough.*

It was another mega-expenditure on behalf of the Company, this time a summit on Corporate Social Responsibility, Safety, Security, and Environment. "The price of gold keeps falling at an uncontrollable rate, projects have been suspended and employees laid off after years of service, and the Company doesn't seem to have a problem with hosting a five-day event for roughly two hundred fifty people in a five-star hotel, including meals and travel costs. Are they seriously mental?" Aline said to herself, standing in line while waiting to check in. Browsing the multi-page agenda for the summit, she shook her head slowly. "You can always count on a Company event to be absurdly packed with back-to-back presentations, workshops, and discussion groups. Hmm. Don't see any space for bathroom breaks. Guess we'll just have to hold it in," she said acerbically.

"Hi, Frank. Already checked in?"

"Yes. I got in last night."

"I've been looking over the program, and it's pretty full. Do you think we'll have a chance to do a bit of shopping?"

"Maybe," he said, smiling.

"You know, the area is famous for outlet malls," he continued. "I rented a minivan just in case."

"Good thinking."

"And I also looked up the best mall. Seems to be Sawgrass Mills, about forty-five minutes away."

"Cool. We can take Lewis and some of the girls from the team, too."

The sun was making its way across the western horizon when Aline arrived at the Company cocktail hour and buffet dinner. The air was warm, and the soft ocean breeze swayed the palm trees gently. The open courtyard of the event was already quite full, with men in comfortable slacks and sport coats, and the ladies in light, playful evening dresses. She spotted Lewis by the bar with a cold beer.

"Hey, what's up?"

"Nothing," he replied pleasantly. "Let me get you a beer."

"For sure. Thanks."

Frank came up behind them. "Hola, hola."

"Would you like a Corona?" Aline asked.

"*Sí*, por favor."

The three turned and faced each other, making a small, tight circle. Aline brought up her bottle. "Here's to a kick-ass security team," she said. "I'm truly proud to be a part of it."

"To the three musketeers," said Lewis.

"A los tres amigos," added Frank as they clinked their bottles together.

The next day began very early, with coffee, tea, and refreshments served in every conference room. Company employees had the opportunity to pop in and out of the different discussions, which were organized according to theme. The room was filled with security members from the Canadian, Mexican, Guatemalan, and Argentinian mines and offices.

"And there you have it, my esteemed colleagues. A day in the life of the Regional Security Team in Mexico," said Aline, whose last comment was met with applause. "Any comments or questions?"

"Well, after listening to your presentation, I'm really glad to be at the mine in northern Ontario," voiced one of her colleagues, a head of security and former police officer. "I think we're just fine dealing with the cold weather and the occasional bear wandering onto the property," he laughed.

A week before Miami, Aline had fittingly attended an interesting book launch concerning the history of narco trafficking in Mexico written by an ex-director of CISEN.[50] The literary soiree—media coverage and all—had the usual assemblage of political figures, embassy officials, heads of law enforcement agencies, guests, and ever-present, inconspicuous, close protection personnel with customary earpieces, dark suits a size or

50 *Centro de Investigación y Seguridad Nacional*—The Center for Research and National Security.

two too small, and pants riding above the ankles, most likely as a preventive measure in case of flooding. And of course, who could miss the unmistakable bulges, not part of any anatomical feature, but the pistols that were moderately tucked away out of sight.

Since Aline had already staked out the entry and exit points of the event, she made an educated guess as to where the author would be coming in. Pre-purchased book in hand, she had studied the author's face—thanks to the inside cover—and was sure that she would recognize him. Pen at the ready, she was the first to spot the ex-head of Mexico's Intelligence Agency.

"Mucho gusto, Aline Belanger," she said, extending her hand in greeting. "I enjoyed your book very much, and I think it gave me a good perspective on the complexity of narco trafficking in the country. Would you be so kind as to sign my copy, please?" she asked, handing him her pen.

"Por supuesto, Aline."

Para Aline con afecto. Qué bueno que
ayudó a comprender a México.

Meanwhile, the irregularities at the Zacatecas mine concerning the Security Department had evolved disproportionately, inciting a deep-dive investigation carried out by an external professional service and auditing firm.

"Okay," said the associate partner. "As mentioned, I will send you the formal engagement letter, and once the mutual NDA is signed, we can kick off the audit."[51]

....

51 NDA—Non-Disclosure Agreement.

"Sounds good. Thank you. Once I receive the document, I will pass it to our Legal Department for review then get it back to you promptly."

As soon as the date was confirmed, Aline opted to dispatch Frank as POC, or point of contact, to receive the auditors on-site. *Less conspicuous than if I were there,* she reflected.

****

In early May, Mr. Straddler, received a polite invitation from top management to move to Vancouver and work out of the head office.

"There's no way that I'm trading my home and property in Alberta for a closet in Vancouver," he said emphatically to Aline over the phone.

"Yeah. That's the price of living in the most expensive city in Canada," she replied.

"Well, I'm gonna say it. They can take this job and shove it."

Aline laughed. "Word," she said, giggling.

"Looks like you're up," he chortled.

"Let's see what happens. I'm not sure I'm willing to make the move to British Columbia."

The following morning, the ex-Mountie formally tendered his resignation with the Company. Soon thereafter, he picked up an assignment as an outsourced security advisor for the Company's number-one competitor, the largest Canadian mining corporation in the world.

A few days later, Aline was sitting at her desk when she received an incoming call from a Vancouver number.

"Hello? This is Aline Belanger."

"Hello, Aline," said the VP of Human Resources in his pleasant voice and distinguished British accent. "How are you?"

"Fine, thank you. And yourself?" Aline always enjoyed talking with the older gentleman in a proper, almost protocol-like manner.

"I am sure that you are aware of the fact that Mr. Straddler has decided to leave the Company."

"Yes, I am."

"Well, top management has requested that I extend an invitation to you so that you may participate in a series of interviews here in the head office if you are interested in the position."

"Yes, of course. Thank you very much. The challenge sounds really exciting."

"Wonderful. I will send out an invite shortly through Outlook. Cheers."

A week later, Aline was preparing for the seven individual interviews that she would endure in Vancouver. The Company's star-studded lineup would include four EVPs—one each from Corporate Affairs, Legal/General Counsel, Capital Management, and Operations—one SVP from Environment & Sustainability, the VP of Human Resources, and an HR manager. *The only one missing is the president & CEO,* she mused.

Her trip happened to coincide with that of her Chilean boss, so they decided to have dinner at a famous local oyster bar. It was packed, with a lot of hustle and bustle. They either had to sit by the bar or stand in line with a large group of people waiting to be seated at tables. Aline hadn't eaten raw oysters before and wasn't sure if they would have any unpleasant effects on her. *Nothing like a potential outbreak or allergic reaction combined with the runs before a series of major interviews,* she thought. Nonetheless, the menu was just too enticing.

"What would you recommend?" she asked.

"Oh, everything is great. I come here all the time, whenever I get the chance," he replied.

"Let the good times roll," Aline said to herself.

As dinner continued, they chatted about work and life in Chile. She liked her boss. He was tranquil and thoughtful, short in stature with long, grey hair and glasses, close to his mid-sixties. *Looks a bit like a weathered roadie waiting to unload and set up equipment for some rock band before a concert,* she mused. *Calm under pressure.* While that quality worked well with crisis management, her boss was known to suffer from a mild case of narcolepsy. Or maybe it was *el mal del puerco,* as Mexicans called it, even though this sleepy condition was limited to presenting itself right after eating, usually a prelude to an afternoon siesta. *Hmm. No. I would lean toward bouts of uncontrollable drowsiness, attributed perhaps to age,* Aline scrutinized. She chortled to herself as her boss ordered a variety of oysters, remembering a recent comment that he had made in his office. "You're like the bulldog of the Company," he said smilingly. Hopefully that meant being considered a protector of the household and not some reference to a physical trait of the canine.

Drizzle outside. "Wouldn't expect anything else from Vancouver," she said, opening an umbrella that was available to guests. The corporate office was about two and a half blocks from the hotel. Aline couldn't resist snapping a selfie in front of the building with the Company name and logo on a directory list made of marble. The night before, she reviewed the personalized written security strategies that she had meticulously prepared for each of the interviewers. She had also conducted a quick background search on each of the executives to bring context to the individualized documents. There was one clear message that Aline put together that she would unfailingly repeat verbatim. In every interview, if the Company intended on maintaining the actual model of corporate security—specifically, a one-person show with no actual support, covering seven countries and approximately fourteen operations and projects—and was furthermore not inclined to make fundamental, necessary changes within the function and scope of work, then she would politely express her gratitude for having been considered for the position and irrevocably decline.

"So, as you can see here in the benchmarking graph, in relation to the number of personnel within any given corporate security structure in the mining sector and across other industries, the Company is currently seriously understaffed to handle operations in an efficient manner. Moreover, it lacks the adequate corporate hierarchy present in other areas," she said to the COO. "I'm not talking about nice-to-have scenarios. This is a focus on bare essentials in alignment with the requirements of the Company's business strategy."

On the flight back to Mexico, Aline kicked back in business class, listening repeatedly to a song played by a Canadian rock band from Alberta. She strummed the chords on the right side of her leg with an imaginary guitar pick while jotting down the lyrics on a napkin, a little tactic she had picked up from her Argentinian guitar tutor, Jiumba—rocker incarnate and musical kindred spirit. The song struck a chord with her; thinking about being away from home, family, and close friends, she recalled the personal introspection that an MGM had shared with her while both of them waited to catch the same flight to Chihuahua.

"Yeah. It's sad when you think about it," he said as they sat in the seats at the boarding gate. "I watched two marriages dissolve because of the mine, and being away so much, I missed out on my daughter. Sure, I talk to her now and again, but we're pretty much estranged," he said softly, breaking off eye contact with her to look somewhere else.

Aline took another sip of ginger ale from the glass she had placed on the open tray in front of her and remembered another heartfelt reflection from a VP at one of the HR sessions in Playa del Carmen. "Regrettably, I wasn't there to see my little girls transform into beautiful and caring young women," he said, teary-eyed.

Remorse, she pondered. *The overwhelming guilt of not seeing your children grow up, not sharing in the little moments of life, like baby teeth falling out or first bike rides and knee scrapes. Not being there for a friend who needed to mend a broken heart or spending quality time with your life partner, talking about nothing.* Aline vowed that she would not let that happen. Ever.

She turned her head and made small talk with a very attractive colleague from the regional office who sat across from her, also in an aisle seat. She was a tall, voluptuous blonde from the Vancouver area with blue eyes and a friendly demeanor.

"So, were you in the head office for meetings?" she asked.

"Yeah, something like that. How about you?"

"Just a couple. Then I took a few days off to spend time with my family and friends."

"That's nice."

"Yeah, it was," she said, sighing.

"Would you like another ginger ale?" asked the stewardess.

"No thanks. I'm fine."

Meanwhile, her colleague got up to go to the lavatory—for a third time, Aline noticed. When she came back, Aline could see that she was a bit pale.

"You okay?" she asked.

"Um, not too good. My stomach is kind of shaky. Must have been the oysters I ate."

"Here," said Aline, handing her a dissolvable Imodium tablet that she had retrieved from her carry-on. "This should help. It takes effect really quickly."

"Thanks so much," her colleague said thoughtfully.

Dozing off, Aline's mind kept going back to the triplet of security incidents that had occurred the previous week. The first was the abduction of an employee from the Guerrero mine. On his way home from work, he was physically extracted at gunpoint from a transport vehicle carrying personnel for apparently being a member of the criminal group that was extorting the community. The second was the kidnapping of the municipal president of Mezcala, and the third, a contractor shot to death by an employee from the Zacatecas mine, who was already in police custody. *Normal week in Mexico,* she thought as everything faded to black.

A week later, she was totally aphonic. For the first time in her life, she wouldn't be able to voice an opinion or comment about something, only managing to muster a soft, almost imperceptible whisper when attempting to speak. Later, this would actually be so comical to Aline that she would laugh out loud recalling the meetings she had during this period, one in particular with the president & CEO and a couple of directors from a company in the energy industry looking to get her take on security and business in the region.

"So, as I mentioned, intelligence has a fundamental role in any successful strategy," she whispered, almost as if they were discussing top-secret matters.

"Okay," said the president, whispering unintentionally. "And who would you actually consider to be the least corrupt entity with respect to the armed forces and law enforcement?" he asked softly.

"Well, you can't really generalize," she answered quietly. "But if I were to make an educated guess, I would say a top-down model—the Army and Navy are okay, then Federal Police. Everything else goes downhill from there."

****

Organizational restructuring again. "Man, I'm getting whiplash from these changes," she said aloud, reading an electronic memorandum from Human Resources.

This time, her Chilean boss, Sleepy, was reassigned to an inferior position within the Company back in Chile. "On the bright side, he's going back to his home country, and his wife will be happy to be living in her own house once more." He was replaced by the former MGM from the Guerrero mine, who would be occupying the recently lowered position of Regional Vice President. Time to break in a new boss again," she sighed. "At least this time I already know him," she said a bit more optimistically.

A month later, she was at the Mayakoba for another five-day team-building workshop. If anyone had started to tally up the number of workshops they had partaken in to build the management team, they would unquestionably conclude that either the team was really, really bad at integration or there were just too many changes among its members. It was obviously the latter. Aline wanted to suggest that they rename the sessions "Team Re-Building," which would have been more accurate. "And the Company just keeps spending and spending on these over-the-top outings," she said disappointedly. "We could have easily carried out the sessions in Mexico City at a fraction of the cost."

It was during the month of August—on the twenty-second, to be exact—that the president of the republic was finally able to implement the concept of a gendarmerie as part of the federal strategy to reduce organized crime in the country.[52] Structurally speaking, the Force would be a division of the Federal

....

52 Gendarmerie (or Gendarmery)—A military force charged with police duties among a civilian population, with jurisdiction in civil law enforcement.

Police under the National Commission of Security and would be deployed to areas where agricultural, mining, and petroleum production were at risk. Unfortunately, the number of officers comprising the ranks would be considerably lower than originally anticipated. Aline would experience the effects of this firsthand in the future when she submitted requests for additional Federal Protection agents as reinforcement for existing sites and Company projects, which were politely turned down, with the response that at the moment, there were no more available officers. What she later found out was that Federal Protection personnel were actually being incorporated into the gendarmerie.

Returning to the office, somewhat disillusioned from her meeting with Federal Protection, the e-mail she had been waiting for from the auditing firm was already in her inbox.

> Dear Aline. We have concluded the investigation and have elaborated a preliminary report, which I would like to discuss with you in private at your earliest convenience. Please let me know when you are available for a meeting in your office. Thank you in advance. Best Regards.

Aline immediately sent out a meeting request, and that same week, she was behind closed doors going over findings with the associate partner who was managing the case file.

Irish-born. Petite with curly blonde hair, green eyes, glasses, and years of experience in Mexico, the associate partner was well versed in investigations dealing with fraud, corruption, money laundering, and other financial crimes.

"Fraud. No doubt about it," she said firmly. "And it's been going on for quite some time now," she observed. "It really comes down to a lack of supervision and control concerning incurred costs within the department."

No need to confirm that finding, said Aline to herself. She had noted in the past that all decisions ended with the head of site security, and even though the position was not management level, he was the sole person responsible for the authorization of all payments for security services. There was no evidence of any regulation with respect to cost center expenses or transparency concerning departmental practices.

Aline clearly recalled the comments made by the MGM and director of Finance in her office when she brought the first few irregularities to their attention. "No. That's impossible," said the MGM. "He's a good soldier and very trustworthy."

"There's no way that he's involved in something," they chimed in, almost indignant at Aline's suggestion.

Going over the preliminary report, they began to list the identified anomalies: invoices for guard services paid to the security provider prior to services rendered; notable discrepancies between the number of actual security personnel on-site and the quantity of guards charged for; fictitious services; and salaries being paid out to the guards in cash with unspecified deductions as opposed to electronic deposits, and special "bonuses" received by the head of security and his 2 I/C for no apparent reason.

"Well, I'm really interested to see the damage in terms of the amount of overbilling," said Aline, flipping to last page of the report. She paused. "Is this right?" she asked, bewildered by the number.

"Yes," answered the associate partner.

"Forty-seven million pesos! Unbelievable. And I am sure, beyond any doubt, that in reality, the amount is significantly higher."[53]

"It is. However, we only presented amounts that could be substantiated with hard, documental evidence."

"Of course. Well, thank you very much. Your company did a very thorough job."

"Thank you," she said as she stood and extended her hand. "As agreed, I will send the formal report to the EVP and general counsel in Vancouver. Have a nice afternoon, Aline."

"Thanks, you too." Aline sat back down in her chair, looking out over the corporate landscape. Two hawks flew by, gently gliding on the warm air currents. People in the office generally referred to them as *águilas*. "Must be searching for prey." She fixed her gaze on no particular point and smiled in satisfaction. The investigation had proven what she had speculated all along.

After the official report was emitted, the same MGM and director of Finance acknowledged to Aline personally that they had been totally duped by the head of security and should have listened to her before the situation escalated.

She took a mouthful of bottled water and felt even more satisfied with the fact that she was able to install an implant at the Zacatecas mine using a person that she requested from the Israeli brothers. Apart from monitoring the Security Department,

53 The estimated amount was more than MXN $80 million.

Aline was following up on rumors of a prostitution ring and the consumption of illegal narcotics within the mine. At the time, Mr. Bozeman had tasked her with finding out if certain female workers were making extra cash for themselves or whether they were part of some organized group that had its own *padrote* who also distributed drugs. The implant was a big guy, muscular with a shaved head and a thick, black moustache. In order to maintain strict confidentiality and guarantee—at least to a certain extent—that there were no ties to any external third party or to Aline herself, he was contracted directly by the mine as a safety officer, whose function allowed him to move about the installations without question. This position reported to Aline directly and in a dotted line, to the new MGM. The former mine general manager had been transferred to the Chihuahua mine.

Unfortunately, within a relatively short amount of time, the covert initiative had to be shut down due to an information leak that prompted her to remove the implant immediately for his own security. By process of elimination, she had rightly deduced that the source of the leak was the new MGM.

"Well, it couldn't have been me," she deliberated, "unless I have multiple personalities and one of them decided to sabotage me. Shh. I think she can hear us. Haha! But seriously, if it wasn't me, the next on my list is my boss, and I'm sure that it wasn't him." He was the only person Aline knew who was so closed-mouthed that he could maintain extensive, endless conversations or answer e-mails with monosyllabic responses like "yes," "no," "done," and "agreed."

"The Israelis? Impossible." Other than the obvious fact that they were both very professional and highly trained ex-military, it was highly unlikely that they would risk losing the lucrative monthly income paid out by the Company for the mini task force services that had expanded to Guerrero, in addition to the continuous special services, which included the implant.

"That leaves me with the MGM. Reminder: secret information *not to be discussed* with MGM or even mentioned when he is in hearing distance."

CHAPTER 8

Late September, two days after Aline's birthday, to be exact, and a news story surfaced that catapulted the security climate of Mexico into the spotlight of international media coverage, setting in motion a series of exhaustive investigations, both national and foreign, that became the focal point of demonstrations and protests that continue to the present: the disappearance of forty-three students from Ayotzinapa, Guerrero.

Sitting at home, Aline watched the weekend news report and listened intently to the details of the developing story that were obviously still very sketchy.

"A significant number of students, also referred to as Normalistas, seemingly went missing yesterday evening after a violent incident in the city of Iguala," said the reporter.[54]

The incident, which would come to be known as the "Iguala Case," began around 6:00 p.m. when a group of students from the Escuela Normal de Ayotzinapa were reported to have taken control of two commercial buses destined for Iguala. At about 9:00 p.m., they were

54 *Normalistas*—Students enrolled in a "normal" school, which is a term used in Spanish to describe a college that trains high school graduates to become teachers.

already in Iguala and had apparently commandeered two more buses.

The news reporter continued, commenting that the Municipal Police of Iguala had reported the situation to the control center of the municipality, per statements from the person on duty at the Civil Protection & Public Security Office. It was assumed that the students had intended to boycott the festivities of the mayor of Iguala and his wife held in the city at that very moment. After receiving information about the unrest, the mayor allegedly requested assistance from the police of the municipality of Cocula.

"The first clash between the students and the police resulted in one student being killed, at which point a smaller part of the group separated from the larger one and attempted to leave the area using a bus. In the confusion, shots were fired erroneously at another transportation vehicle carrying a soccer team. Minutes later, the first bus that was seized had been detained, and the students were taken into custody and transported to the Police Central in Iguala. In the meantime, the sub-chief of police from Cocula was dispatched to Iguala. The students were then supposedly corralled into the back of a local transport truck that drove off, leaving no further information as to their whereabouts."

Aline followed the ensuing reports and media coverage closely, with assembled panel experts speculating over the matter and presenting hypotheses of mass executions and burials in clandestine pits seemingly linked to organized crime, and possibly to officials in Iguala. Articles in local newspapers even went so far as to claim that the Company's interests had something to do with the disappearance of the *Normalistas*. There were protests and demonstrations. Highway toll booths were overtaken to allow free passage to motorists as heavily armed military and law enforcement looked on. Formal appeals to the government were made by the parents of the students, demanding immediate intervention and the return of their children, along with pleas to international media and human rights organizations, all while forensic investigations of potential evidence were organized and carried out. Mayhem.

On Friday evening, a couple of weeks after the initial reports of the incident, a group of the students' parents approached the main gate of the Guerrero mine, demanding to search the grounds. They had supposedly been informed that the bodies of the *Normalistas* were buried within the property lines. Joe L. quickly called Aline on her cell phone, nervously requesting orders.

"There's a mob of people here, and they are very angry and hostile," he stammered. "What should we do?"

Aline responded in a calm, reassuring, and confident manner. "I need you to identify the spokesperson of the group. Once you have done so, present yourself and your charge, and calmly inform that person that a small number of people from the group will be granted access to the installations, and they will be able to conduct any search they deem fit in the accompaniment of a few security officers. I want you to be there as a representative of the area and try to facilitate anything within reason. I will be on standby for any additional support that you may require. It's your game, and you're in control," she said.

Having regained his composure, he hung up and carried out her instructions to the letter. "Good for him," she thought while dialing her direct boss. A few hours later, having been satisfied that there were no bodies buried in the mine, the committee of parents left the installations peacefully.

Within a month, the group returned.

"Go ahead," said Aline, identifying the cell phone number of Joe L.

"The parents are back," he said. "This time they're avowing that the students were being held against their will and forced to work in the underground mine." Aline gave him authorization to once again select a representative number from the group and calmly escort them to the mine so that they could attest once and for all that the Company was in no way or form involved in the case of the missing students.

Aline sincerely empathized with the parents' plight, understanding their desperation and feelings of hopelessness in trying to find their children and bring them home.

The Federal Procurement Office continued with its investigation. Pressure was mounting to find the guilty parties. Several allegations were brought to light, including possible collusion with Organized Crime, leading to the arrest and incarceration of the mayor of Iguala, his wife, and a number of police officials in relation to the disappearance of the students. In the midst of the turmoil, the governor of Guerrero resigned from his post, apparently to—in his words—create a more favorable political climate that could bring about a solution to the crisis. He was replaced by an interim governor.

****

In early October, there was a new kid on the block, so to speak. Aline surmised that even though her interviews had gone well with Top Management in Vancouver, the organization was not ready to make the necessary changes to improve the current corporate security function. In a short time, they had hired a new director of Corporate Security, who came from precisely the same corporation where Aline's ex-boss was now consulting. A very slim, medium-height, bearded, and scruffy-looking guy with glasses, Miro was an ex-naval officer from Peru. At his former company, he held the position of director in a group of approximately ten to twelve other security directors. Without ever having had a regional charge, he was only two to three years shy of legal retirement. Aline deduced that this was probably a good position to end his professional career in and most likely the reason he accepted the job.

Aline knew that another regional tour with her new *jefe* was about to commence. Sure enough, the second week of October, they began with the Guerrero mine. The night was warm and filled with serenades of automatic gunfire in the distance. Disconcerting and downright frightening. She could see on Miro's face that he wasn't accustomed to this type of setting.

Morning couldn't have come soon enough. Breakfast in the mine's small canteen was quick, and they were soon on their way to the airstrip, escorted by Federal Protection. Next stop, Cuernavaca, and from there, the Chihuahua mine.

Arriving in the city of Chihuahua, they grabbed an authorized taxi at the airport and headed to their hotel. Aline went to her room to freshen up. She and Miro sat down to dinner and talked security. Aline listened attentively, as she wanted to make sure that she understood what her new boss was expecting from her and the security team in the region.

"As I see it," said Miro, taking another bite of his steak, "we really need to have an integrated regional team." *Okay,* she thought. *Not too insightful, but maybe he's just breaking the ice.*

At 6:00 a.m., a hotel shuttle was ready, with its engine running, to take them to the hangar at the airport where they would board a flight to El Fuerte, Sinaloa. Snoozing whenever possible and appropriate, Aline opened her eyes as the plane's tires made contact with the tarmac at the rural airport. A number of passengers, mostly mine employees and a couple of visitors, were already standing by to board the plane.

Flying into the Chihuahua mine airspace, all of Aline's somnolence had dissipated. She felt nervous. Unrest in the region between conflicting groups had escalated into brutal exchanges. Recently, one group utilized a Barrett .50 caliber sniper rifle to bring down a small aircraft, killing all passengers, who happened to be rival family members trying to escape from the region.[55] *Wouldn't want to be the victim of mistaken identity,* Aline thought, somewhat concerned.

....

55 The effective firing range of the Barrett .50 caliber rifle is approximately 1.8 kilometers.

When the plane landed, they were received by the new manager of security at the Chihuahua mine. Aline presented him to Miro and then threw her backpack into the open pickup. Lewis walked up to them.

"Hello," he said. He had arrived the day before to discuss some operational matters with site security.

Arriving at the administration building, they walked toward the MGM's office, stopping at a kitchenette to have coffee and little sandwiches with some of the employees. Aline was always touched by the camaraderie of the people at this particular mine. Perhaps it was a by-product of the location's utter isolation, long work days, and shared, after-hours activities, like barbecues, sporting events, and Friday night dances. It had a very familial feeling to it, with momentary, almost carefree, relaxing sensations at times, even stirring emotions of nostalgia. *Quite the paradox,* she reflected, *considering that we are situated right smack in the middle of an extremely dangerous, potentially life-threatening environment.*

After the meeting with the MGM, they set up in one of the boardrooms and worked from there until dinnertime. Cleaning up at the hand-washing stations, they entered the canteen. Bandamax was on the tube, as expected, only to be changed to *El Chavo del Ocho*.[56] During dinner, Aline's boss turned around in his seat unexpectedly, and startlingly addressed the security supervisor seated at the next table.

....

56 *El Chavo del Ocho*—An enormously popular Mexican TV sitcom from the mid-1970s featuring adults in the roles of small children that continues to be aired to the present day.

"¿Qué onda, maricón? ¿Cómo va?" he asked, not waiting for a response. His questions were followed by bursts of uncontrollable cackling. At first, Aline thought that he may have been suffering from some type of mental disorder that impeded him from controlling what came out of his mouth, but this was quickly discarded because of the lucidity of his other comments and conduct in general. She looked furtively at Lewis, who also shared the same expression of disbelief. Those types of comments could land you a beating really fast from someone who might not appreciate that type of sense of humor, particularly between miners.

Glad to be on her way to the room, Aline washed her face and brushed her teeth, collapsing into bed. She was asleep before her head hit the pillow. The next morning, she made her way sleepily to the bathroom and turned on the light. As she stood in the shower rinsing out shampoo, out of the corner of her eye she perceived a slight movement a few inches from her feet. Scorpion. Transparent. Striped, honey-like color, venomous. Side-stepping the creature while keeping an eye on it at all times, she reached for her sandal and cell phone that was close by, wanting some evidence for posterity's sake.

"Sorry, amigo. It's you or me," she said. Even though Aline was generally fond of animals, the thought of being stung and having to wait for either the next incoming flight or traveling several hours via road to get to a medical facility was not an option. She carried out the process swiftly and efficiently.

The security supervisor was outside, waiting to accompany her to breakfast.

"Buenos días. How did you sleep?" he asked.

"Buenos días. Fine. I did have an unexpected guest in the shower, though," she said sardonically.

"Alacrán?"

"Yup." He paused, thinking. "I guess we should program the next fumigation for the rooms." *Yeah, good idea,* she thought, biting her tongue.

Seat belts were fastened, and they were ready for takeoff. *Here we go again.* Aline thought about whether it would be feasible to paint the Company aircrafts with some distinct, bright, and fluorescent color that would make them easily identifiable as mine aircraft and therefore less likely to be shot down by Organized Crime, at least from a close distance.

Airborne, with no incident to report, they flew to Cedros, Zacatecas about two hours and twenty minutes away. No sooner had they landed than they stepped into a security pickup truck and headed north to the locality of Matamoros to review the security measures for a well field project.[57]

An hour later, they arrived and were received by the newly hired security supervisor for the project. In the middle of nowhere. Literally. Scorching heat and incessant dust blowing. At first glance, the compound had a bit of a trailer-park look to it—fenced-in, portable-like structures with two to three steps leading up to the doors of each compartment, and small but clean living quarters for personnel with satellite TV hookup.

....

57 Well field project—An area containing one or more wells that produce usable amounts of water.

After a couple of hours, they had completed the security review and headed back to the mine to spend the night.

"I'll stop by your room at 6:00 a.m. sharp to pick you up so we can head to the project in San Tiburcio," she said to her boss.

"Sounds good to me."

It was still dark, and the air was cool the next morning when Aline closed the door behind her and started to walk toward the one-story building where her boss was lodged. The streets between the employee housing units were paved, and each corner had a stop sign. To the left, she could see the outline of the constructed chapel, and in front, at a distance, were large eating halls and administrative buildings. It reminded her of a little suburban community. As she neared the external door to her boss's room, the security coordinator from the project they were about to visit pulled up and parked his pickup.

"Buenos días, Aline," said Danny.

"Hola. Buenos días." Aline climbed the short steps and knocked on the door. No answer. She waited a few seconds, then knocked again. Still nothing. Looking down at her Luminox tactical watch, which was luminescent in the darkness, she checked to make sure that she hadn't been too zealous, arriving earlier than scheduled. Nope. It was now 6:04 a.m. She knocked once again, this time more energetically. Footsteps and someone bumping into things could be heard. Her boss opened the door a crack. He was shirtless, with his hair in disarray and eyes half-closed.

"What's up? What's happening?"

"It's time to leave for the project, sir," she replied, trying not to sound too annoyed and irritated.

"Oh right, the project. I'll be right out," he said, closing the door and shuffling off.

WTF, she thought. She stopped in her tracks, instinctively raising her hand to cover her mouth, wondering whether she had said that out loud.

As she sat in the passenger seat of the truck, she tried to think of something a bit more pleasant than the situation at hand. Aline had been recently invited to collaborate with the Enterprise Risk Management Department, or ERM, and specifically take on the role of the Company's "Risk Champion" in Mexico.

"Thank you very much," she had said enthusiastically to the ERM manager over the phone. "And I can also see this as a great opportunity for the Security Departments across all of the regions of operation to better align themselves with the Company's risk framework."

"Absolutely, Aline. And you heading up the initiative in Mexico will make it just so much easier," said the manager. "I'm really glad you're on board, and I look forward to working with you."

The drive to the project was pretty quiet, as her boss slept the entire trip, with an occasional loud snore that confirmed that he was still out.

"So, how are things at the project, Danny?" she asked.

He looked up into the rearview mirror to see if Miro was still asleep, then answered in a hushed tone. "People are really nervous about the rumors of the project being shut down and losing their jobs, including myself. Have you heard anything about it at the regional office?"

Aline trusted Danny and never had a reason to doubt his discretion. When she had interviewed him for the position, what caught her attention on his curriculum vitae was the fact that he had studied at a monastery to become a priest, eventually adjusting his career path toward the mining industry.

"Well, I haven't heard anything specific about a date or any announcement that the project will be shut down indefinitely. Nevertheless, with the price of gold where it is, I know that Top Management is scrambling to look for alternatives."

"So, what could you imagine happening?"

"I would look at it this way. They can't influence the price of gold. It is what it is. So logically, they will start looking to divest with respect to projects and focus on consolidating the moneymaker of the region, which is clearly the Zacatecas mine."[58]

On-site at the project, Aline and the new director were hustled into a large meeting room where the majority of the administration staff was politely waiting to receive them.

"Hola, Aline," said the general manager, greeting her warmly with a friendly hug. "¿Cómo has estado?"

"Muy bien. Muchas gracias," Aline said, smiling. "Te presento a mi nuevo jefe." She gestured at her boss and stepped out of the way.

"Buenos días, mucho gusto. I am the general manager of this project."

"Mucho gusto. I am the new director of Corporate Security from the head office in Vancouver."

....

58 At the time, the Zacatecas mine was already producing close to 620,000 ounces of gold per year.

"Ah. The new Mr. Straddler," he winked.

"*Sí*, only a bit smaller, or maybe a petite version," laughed Miro.

They talked of security measures and collaboration, the importance of following security recommendations, and of having direct communication when in need of orientation or assistance. After the meeting, they were given a tour of the installations and discussed mineral concentrate, housing, and transportation.

In the early afternoon, they got back into the pickup and headed in the direction of the mine. Afterward, they went onward to the Cedros airstrip to catch their flight to Toluca, and from there, drive back to Mexico City.

The next day at the office, they had some internal meetings with the team and then went out to a nearby Seattle-based coffee shop. There was the usual queue to order. Aline looked over the mugs and other items that were strategically placed for customers to see while waiting. When they got to the cashier, Lewis ordered the rounds of java, finishing off the list with his own: *un latte grande, con leche deslactosada y Splenda*.

Aline speedily looked up from her cell phone as she heard the order, looking for the anticipated reaction from her boss. True to his nature, before Lewis had handed over the money to the cashier, her boss exclaimed aloud, "Sure you don't want anything else with that señorita's drink?" He ended the question with his patented, irrepressible cackling attack, eliciting stares of disbelief from a number of persons within earshot. Looking at Frank, who was arranging napkins at the side counter, pretending not to have heard the crass comment, Aline turned around slightly, distancing herself from her boss so as not to be held guilty by association.

As they took their seats at a small table, Aline was glad that most of the people who had been in line had taken their coffees to go.

"So, what do you think about the security situation in Guerrero, Frank?" asked her boss.

"Well, it's a pretty complicated matter, with the fact that different criminal groups keep trying to overthrow one another to gain control of the drug-trafficking routes in the region. Not to mention," he continued, "the rampant corruption, hidden political agendas, Army, Navy, and Federal Police operations, and auto-defense groups."

"No sabes nada, Frank," said her boss in a serious tone before bursting into uncontrollable laughter again. Finishing their beverages, they started walking down Avenida Palmas back toward the office.

Miro's cell phone rang loudly.

"Hello? *Sí*. Just give me a minute," he said, covering his cell. "I have to take this. I'll catch up with you guys in the office."

They continued at a comfortable pace. "Any thoughts on our illustrious boss?" asked Aline ironically.

"Well, I apparently like señorita drinks," said Lewis.

"And I don't know anything about anything," added Frank. They all laughed hysterically.

Aline's cell vibrated. It was an incoming text message from an anonymous number.

Iglesia Covadonga. 10 min. Confesionario.

Nothing like being watched, she thought.

“Hey, I need to take out some cash from the Banamex ATM across the street. I’ll see you in a while,” she said to the guys. Crossing the busy avenue, she headed toward the bank, making sure to walk at a slower pace than her colleagues, who eventually entered the corporate building. Continuing past the cash machine, she turned right onto Calle Sierra Gamón and entered the church from a side door.

The air was cool inside and quite refreshing, a welcome comfort from the heat and sun. Dipping the points of her fingers into the stoup, Aline made the sign of the cross and stepped toward the confessionals, noting that the church was completely empty, as if this had somehow been arranged. She approached the cabinet, which had a small green light above it, meaning “unoccupied.” She opened the door and entered. Kneeling down, she crossed herself.

“Bendígame Padre por que he pecado,” she recited.

“Buenas tardes, hija,” said the voice behind the partition. Opening the panel no more than an inch, he handed her an envelope. “I was given this and instructed to make sure that you, and only you, received it directly from my hand.”

“Gracias, Padre,” she said softly, somewhat confounded by the situation.

“Vaya con Dios, Aline.”

CHAPTER 9

Arriving at her apartment that evening, Aline opened the sealed envelope. "No large sums of cash this time," she sneered jokingly. The envelope was far too thin. Pulling out a Benchmade stiletto automatic switchblade from a drawer nearby, she opened the envelope with surgical precision. Document, ID, credit card, Post-it, and slim, portable flash drive with hardware-based encryption to safeguard data. The paper was an official, one-page, temporary permit dated for the following week issued by SAT to enter the customs area at the AICM, Mexico City's International Airport.[59] She immediately discerned that the identification was a forgery of an IFE card, as it had her photo and a bogus name on it.[60]

"Really professional work. Almost more authentic-looking than the real thing." And the credit card, false, with the same name. She picked up the yellow sticker note and read the short message:

....

59 SAT—*Servicio de Administración Tributaria.* In English, this is the Tax Administration Service under the Secretary of Finance and Public Credit; AICM—*Aeropuerto Internacional de la Ciudad de México.*

60 IFE—*Instituto Federal Electoral,* which is an official photo identification from the former Federal Electoral Institute.

Lunes. 20:00 horas. Aduana. Beltrán-Castro.

"Buenas noches, señorita. ¿A dónde va?" asked the chubby cab driver, leaning on the front of his pink-and-white-painted Nissan Tsuru as he finished off a taco from a street vendor.

"A la aduana del aeropuerto, por favor."

The sun was setting as they drove off in heavy traffic toward the airport about forty-five minutes away.

Pulling up to the main pedestrian entry point of the customs area, the taxi stopped, and Aline got out.

"Muchas gracias, señor. Aquí tiene," said Aline, handing him the fare.

"Gracias. Hasta luego."

Walking to the guardhouse, she took out the access permit.

"Hola. Buenas noches. I have a meeting with Mr. Beltrán-Castro," she said politely.

"Buenas noches, señorita," replied the guard, looking over the document.

"Su IFE, por favor." When Aline handed over her card, he said, "Thank you. One moment, please." He turned to his colleague inside, who picked up the phone to make a call. A couple of minutes later, the first guard stepped back out with a temporary visitor ID in his hand.

"Here you go, señorita. Mr. Beltrán-Castro will be here shortly to receive you."

"Muchas gracias," Aline said with a smile. From a distance, she could see a short, hefty fellow with a thick moustache wearing a shirt and tie driving a golf cart with a roof, making his way toward her. As he drove up, she noticed he was sweating profusely, perspiration trickling down the sides of his head and characteristic sweat patches under both armpits.

"Buenas noches, señorita. Soy el Licenciado Beltrán-Castro, el Administrador de la Aduana, del Aeropuerto Internacional de la Ciudad de México."[61] Aline climbed aboard the cart, and they drove off. To the left, she could see an anthill of workers bustling around, packaging all sorts of material and equipment onto large pallets, while others directed traffic and communicated via radio. Further on, a vehicle completely covered with tarp and steel cords locked into place was being loaded into the cargo hold of an airplane while the corresponding automotive company security staff ensured that there was no breach of confidentiality, per standard protocol for prototype protection.

"Would you like a beverage, señorita?" asked Beltrán-Castro, offering her a can of cola while looking down at her legs.

"No, muchas gracias, Licenciado. I just finished one a while back."

"We are now entering a zone where there is a total blind spot for all of the CCTV cameras," he said, slowing down the electric vehicle. "Do you have the list of accounts that I was promised?" Inferring that he meant the portable memory stick, she reached into her purse and gave it to him.

"Of course. Here you go."

••••••••••••••••••

61 *Licenciado or Lic.*—An academic title used by lawyers and others with a bachelor's degree in many different fields of study, usually affixed before a person's name in documents and/or verbal presentations.

"Muy bien," he said contentedly. Speeding up, they drove for another five minutes, distancing themselves from the previous, open-patio commotion. Aline could see and hear low-flying cargo planes taking off for unknown destinations as they neared a relatively secluded hangar on the left. The immense doors were open, and a small group of personnel was moving hurriedly to load a heavy pallet onto a plane. Now about twenty meters from the bay, the administrator slowed down again.

"Please take note that the cargo is being loaded as per agreement."

"*Sí*, gracias," she replied, watching as the ground crew completed their task and exited the aircraft, the ramp door closing. He pulled over to the side at a maintenance station, and without losing eye contact, she observed the aircraft revving its engines, slowly making its way to the nearest runway. After waiting for a few minutes to receive clearance, it began to taxi down the airstrip, picking up speed and taking off into the dark sky. *Visual confirmation achieved.*

"Ya está," he said, putting the vehicle into motion.

****

One hundred ninety-seven. The number of registered security incidents that Aline had handled since working for the Company. She was tired. Brutally exhausted, actually.

It was early November, and Aline was flying to the Guerrero mine for an internal Remembrance Day, a ceremony for colleagues who had lost their lives in accidents suffered at the Corporation's mines within the last year, two of which occurred in Mexico. The mines coordinated a moment of silence across all time zones and regions.

Aline was also there to look into a disconcerting matter that had come to her attention—the finding of Tovex explosives by military personnel that were discarded on a federal highway near the mine.[62] She recalled the recent phone call she received from Joe L. at about 3:45 p.m.

"Buenas tardes, Aline. I just finished a conversation at Gate 5 with an Infantry lieutenant from the military zone about a box of explosive artifacts, Tovex 100, that they found while carrying out a security patrol on Federal Highway Iguala-Chilpancingo at kilometer one sixty-two, approximately one hundred and fifty sausage-like cartridges that could be from the mine."

Great...not, she said to herself. "Okay. Please arrange to have all of the pertinent information available in terms of procedures, photographs, registries, authorizations, inventory, etcetera when I arrive on-site," she ordered. "Enterado."

After the ceremony, Aline and Joe L. drove down to the security office, talking about the explosives incident.

"So, what did the lieutenant say, extra-officially?" Aline asked.

"He said that they had received an anonymous tip from a truck driver about the box of Tovex."

....

62 Tovex—A water-gel explosive used in mining that has many advantages over dynamite, including lower toxicity and safer manufacture, transport, and storage.

"Well, the good thing is that they approached the mine to find out whether it belonged to the Company or not. And did they tell you which authorities were involved in the discovery of the explosives?" she continued.

"Yes. Apart from the military officers, there were agents from the Federal Police and the Federal Public Ministry from Iguala."

"All right. Let's start by looking at the documents that I requested," Aline said, stepping out of the pickup.

They entered the office and began to go over the paperwork. Drinking from her bottle of water, Aline read the mine's explosives procedure and flow chart elaborated by the warehouse.

"Okay. At least the documents discuss the procedure for handling and safeguarding explosives, which would definitely be useful if an external investigation came up. We do, however, need to verify whether they are actually being applied in day-to-day operations. Please take note of that."

After a couple of hours on the paper trail—and one turkey-breast sandwich later—Aline stopped at a particular shipment order and invoice from four months back.

"Well...unfortunately, here it is," Aline said aloud. "The serial numbers on the explosives that were found coincide with a batch from a shipment received, confirming without a doubt that the artifacts encountered did in fact originate from the mine."

Joe L. was on the phone. "Okay, gracias," he said, hanging up the call. "As you requested, the warehouse manager is on his way with the Inventory, Consolidation

& Consumption documents relating to the Tovex 100, one-inch by eight-inch explosive cartridges."

After a short while, footsteps could be heard on the gravel path leading to the stairs of the office. Knocking on the door, the manager stepped inside.

"Buenas tardes, soy el gerente de almacén," he said.

"Mucho gusto. Aline Belanger. Seguridad." Getting right down to the matter at hand, Aline asked, "Could you please give us a summary concerning the explosives in question and the internal supply process in general?" she asked.

"Por supuesto. The Tovex 100 explosive that we use in the underground mine is considered inert in and of itself because it requires a blasting cap to initiate an explosive reaction. The chemical composition—hydrogel—is also considered stable and resistant to water."

"Good to know. And the process?"

"The explosives are supplied to the U.G. mine from the powder magazine according to kilograms requested, as opposed to a specific number of Tovex 100 units."

"So, just to understand, during any blasting operation, it would be impossible to ascertain if a specific cartridge was used, correct?"

"Yes. The corresponding logs and registries only list the weight of the provisioned explosives," replied the manager.

"And are all of the explosives requested utilized at one time?"

"Um, no," he said hesitantly.

"So what happens to the explosives that are not consumed?"

"The artifacts not used from a previous work shift are housed in temporary storage areas within the U.G. mine itself and are not returned to the powder magazine. They are carried over to the next shift." *First major gap detected.*

"Is this provisional housing under lock and key with limited access?"

The manager sighed. "No. The areas are open and uncontrolled."

Looking over at Joe L., Aline asked, "Do security personnel check individuals when they leave the U.G. mine after completing their shift?"

Clearing his throat a bit, the security superintendent answered, "No, they don't." *Second gap.*

"Okay. We can now surmise that the lack of a security search and seizure point during shift changes in the U.G. mine, coupled with the open temporary storage areas for carry-over explosives, would easily facilitate the extraction of the artifacts." Sitting back in her chair and clasping her hands behind her head, she continued. "So, we have the potential how. All we need to determine is the who, when, and more importantly, the why. Let's go back to the documents," she said, leaning forward.

About twenty minutes of pretty much silence went by until Aline spoke again. "If we look at the volume of explosives ordered from the supplier, estimate the quantity consumed per shift, and take into consideration the dates between the order the batch came from and the following order received, we can pretty accurately deduce that the Tovex 100 artifacts were removed from the U.G. mine sometime around two to three weeks after the shipment first arrived."

“Makes sense,” said the warehouse manager.

“Well, thanks very much for the input and your time. If we need anything else, we’ll be sure to contact you,” Aline said, extending her hand.

“Mucho gusto, Señorita Aline.”

“Why don’t we stretch our legs a bit and walk for a while?” she said to Joe L.

“Yes, I like that idea.”

They stepped out into the hot air and ambled in front of the entrance to the U.G. mine. She looked at him and, lowering her voice—even though there was no one around—said, “You know, I contacted the corporate office of the explosives supplier to receive the exact cost per Tovex 100 unit, and I was really surprised that it is relatively inexpensive, so that discards the hypothesis that the explosives were stolen for resale on the black market. It’s just not viable economically speaking, in comparison to, for example, illegal firearms. And as the warehouse manager mentioned, the artifacts require additional items, like blasting caps, to initiate the explosive process.”

“You’re right. There are plenty of other things that can be sold with less hassle.” Stopping, Joe L. turned to her. “You know that I was born in Guerrero, right?”

“Yes, of course. I remember you mentioning it before.”

“Well, I recall hearing that local residents in this area have been known to use these types of explosives in small amounts for fishing purposes since it is far more efficient and effective than using a fishing rod.”

“It’s plausible, although I would think that if it were just for a fishing excursion, then maybe two or three units of the explosive would be enough. One hundred and fifty pieces would probably be considered overkill. We can also rule out the idea that Organized Crime would be interested in the explosives since there are readily available devices, like fragment grenades, that detonate without the entire process required for Tovex 100 detonation."

"Agreed," he said. "And as I think about it, whoever took the explosives, or as the case may be, received them from someone who had access to the storage area, they might have been transporting them in an open pickup-type vehicle or truck where the artifacts could have just fallen off without anyone even noticing it. It strikes me as a bit unusual that someone would just dump a box of explosives on the side of the road in public view. You could easily find a place to dispose of them without having to worry about witnesses."

"Okay. So then I'll write up the report with our findings and the measures we can implement to improve controls in the process and send it to Corporate Security."

****

Saturday night in the municipality of Azcapotzalco, Mexico City. Not for the faint of heart, at least after sundown. Aline was heading out to listen to live metal and hard rock music at a local bar upon invitation from her rocker tutor, who was celebrating his birthday. She slipped into some jeans, a black T-shirt, leather jacket, and mining boots, just in case someone got out of line and needed a reminder to behave, courtesy of steel-toed footwear. Metal cross hanging around her neck, a wrist chain, and a skull ring on her finger, she knew that she would be able to blend in.

With music pounding and guitar riffs sounding, she made her way up the narrow, dimly lit stairwell to the second-floor bar. The cover was fifty pesos. It was so dark and dirty, Aline wasn't sure if "bar" was the appropriate term for the establishment. Perhaps "drinking hole" would have captured the essence a bit better. *Awesome.* It reminded her of a nightclub in downtown Toronto on Queen Street West that she had strolled into on one occasion. It was called "Sanctuary: The Vampire Sex Bar," a misnomer, as the bar was far from fulfilling the scope of its name—no vampires, and no sex for that matter—just gothic folk with black hair, dark lipstick, Doc Marten boots, and bodies grinding away to industrial electronic music.

The only difference here was the genre—tattooed bikers and patrons garbed in chains, leather, and boots; raunchy chicks; waitresses with pierced tongues and eyebrows wearing ripped jeans or hiked-up skirts; and of course, who could miss the standard thug or two confined to the darker corner tables, if more darkness was even possible. Feeling inside her jacket, all she found were her house keys. *Should have brought my brass knuckles*. There was a local band onstage churning out a thrash-metal melody with guttural vocals, gyrations, and long-hair swaying. *Bitchin'*.

"Hola. ¿Algo de tomar?" asked a petite server in a tight T-shirt and cute nose ring.

"Una Corona, por favor." Laughing to herself, Aline wanted to add the cliché, "Yeah, and make sure it comes in a dirty glass," but she knew that it would get lost in translation.

The restrooms were a bit cramped with little to no light. *Good thing I'm sitting down to pee, or things could get messy,* she thought. Returning to her table, the Argentinian hit the stage with his band named Again, the music shifting from heavy metal to '80s and '90s rock tunes.

Aline swayed her head slowly to the rhythm and slugged back another beer, thinking about the sudden and unexpected resignation of the MGM from the Zacatecas mine. The publicized version was that someone had witnessed him violating a Golden Rule by driving a utility vehicle at the mine without a seat belt and that *he* had made the decision to leave the Company because he could no longer be a role model of safety for the mine employees. *Bullshit.* She found this absurdly hard to believe since there was a recent report emitted concerning the newly appointed VP of Health & Safety from the Vancouver office. She had blatantly violated the exact same rule during a visit to the underground mine in Guerrero. However, in her case, there was no disciplinary action whatsoever.

"Muchísimas gracias. And now, I'd like to bring up a special friend to play something for you. Aline, por favor." Snapping out of her trance, Aline looked up, then quickly scanned the place for an escape route, only to find a small balcony. *Two-story jump. Not that bad,* she considered.

"Vamos. Un aplauso para la señorita," he said into the mic. The crowd clapped and cheered in support. Stepping up onto the stage, she moved in close to him. "I'm going to kill you for this," she said in a low tone, covering the microphone with her hand. He smiled and handed her a white ESP Eclipse guitar, which she slung over her shoulder. Then she pulled out a pick from the small change pocket of her jeans.

"¿Te parece algo de Audioslave?" he asked.

"Claro, por supuesto," she said, thinking of the only song they had rehearsed together from the iconic group. She quickly tried to remember where the guitar solo started. *Was it the fifteenth or seventeenth fret?*

****

Before the end of the first quarter of the new year, Aline's direct boss, the regional VP and former MGM of the Guerrero mine, informed the executive team that he was leaving the Company after eleven years of dedicated service. Observing his facial expression and breathing pattern, Aline knew that this was not of his own accord. There were only two plausible scenarios: either he had done something that was frowned upon by the Company, or they had decided to write him out of the script, just like that. In this case, it would most likely be the latter. Aline would never come to know the exact details. However, her intuition—and the fact that she had seen at least five high-level executives in the region become victims of the same circumstances—told her that there was a pretty good chance that she was right. Her now ex-boss would be replaced by a hard-core veteran miner ascending to the once-again, newly open position of regional SVP focused on one bottom-line directive: the production of gold.

He was an older chap, a big guy with a serious yet calm bearing who spoke two to three times slower than normal, which Aline would eventually find exasperating. He looked worn out and tired. Perhaps this was the toll exacted by many years of arduous work in the mining industry. As his obstinate mindset was exclusively production-driven, he would demonstrate a continuous disregard for—and lack of interest in—the other areas of the Company, particularly Security and Community Relations. In short order, both areas would be restructured in terms of direct-line reporting.

During a visit to the regional office, the executive vice president of Corporate Affairs came into Aline's office to inform her about departmental restructuring.

"And so, just to make sure that you hear it from the source, as of Monday you will be reporting to Woody, the director of Corporate Affairs, and no longer to the regional SVP."

"All right then," she said in acknowledgement. "Thank you for the information." *Makes sense,* she thought, *considering that the regional SVP cannot be bothered with the security of the Company's personnel in the region, what with his singular interest being the increase of gold production.*

****

It was mid-March, and Aline had been invited to speak at the Shale World Mexico Summit on creating a guideline for a risk management strategy in Mexico. It yielded a big turnout, including many C-Suite executives from various industries, including a few Scandinavian companies from the energy sector who were looking to conduct business in Mexico.[63]

....

63 C-Suite Executives—Slang term used to collectively refer to a corporation's highest-level senior executives (e.g., CEO, CFO, COO).

Aline wanted to share her experience with the audience, citing real-life tactics that could be utilized to mitigate risk and add to the sustainability of any company. She stepped up to the podium and adjusted the mic confidently. Not requiring any notes or papers outlining what she wanted to say, she looked around the room thoughtfully, making eye contact with the audience.

"Ladies and Gentlemen. I'm here to share with you my experiences navigating the complexities of doing business in Mexico through the implementation of a comprehensive risk management strategy. My objective here today is that you take away with you something that you can apply within your own companies."

Looking at the small monitor below in front of the stage, she cued the designated event person to begin advancing the slides of her presentation.

"Risk. No matter how we define it, we know that it can impact our organizations. How we manage it could make the difference between sinking and moving ahead to new horizons. There are five facets that I would consider fundamental to any risk management design. The first is a company's approach to risk itself—whether mitigating, avoiding, transferring, or accepting it—and the subsequent alignment to business strategy. Secondly, stakeholder mapping and engagement, followed by an adequate setup concerning operations made up of public and private security. Fourth, would be information gathering, analysis, and application, and finally, the importance of liaising with state and federal entities."

CHAPTER 10

Polanco. Mexico City. Aline stepped out of the cab in front of the JW Marriott Hotel and walked up the steps to the side entrance of the Club de Industriales, a private, prestigious business club open to members and special invites only. She waited to register and watched as a gentleman before her tried to enter à la Tony Blair.[64]

"Disculpe, señor. Una corbata es obligatoria," said the attendant, impeding the man from reaching the elevators. "But I don't have one," he retorted nervously.

"No worries," she said, reaching for a mahogany box. She opened it to reveal an assortment of four to five ties. "Please select one to your liking." *Now that's client service,* observed Aline.

"Buenas noches, señorita. ¿Su nombre?"

"Aline Belanger. I have a dinner meeting in Salón Puebla."

"One moment, please," said the attendant, checking the guest list.

....

64 Tony Blair—A British politician who served as the prime minister of the United Kingdom and is known for attending functions in a suit and shirt with no necktie. A fan of the "tie-less" look, he was in fact the only modern British prime minister to appear in an official portrait without a tie.

"Yes, of course. Right this way." She escorted Aline to the elevator. "It is on the second floor."

"Muchas gracias."

Baroque music played softly in the background as she walked to the private dining room. It was one of her favorite pieces—Vivaldi's Four Seasons. Teniente was seated facing the door. He stood from his chair as she entered.

"Buenas noches, Aline. Gusto verte."

"Igualmente. Muchas gracias."

"The specialty of the house is delicious this evening. I have taken the liberty of ordering our dinner in advance, if that is all right with you."

"Most certainly," she said, sitting down to his right side so that she could monitor the door for whatever reason there might be to do so. She quietly noticed that he was wearing El Coyote's ring on his right pinky finger.

"Buenas noches, señorita. Perhaps a little vino tinto?"

"*Sí*, por favor. Gracias."

"So, I have been reading that the price of gold is taking a serious hit and dropping uncontrollably. Unfortunate, no?" asked Teniente.

"Yes, I guess so..."

"Well, you don't have to worry about that now, do you?"

"No," she said, flashing a little smile. "So, why the urgency and insistence with this dinner?" queried Aline. She noted the stern look in his eyes.

"I have recently become aware that someone in our organization es un traidor," he said seethingly, as if the words were venom. "Puta madre!" he exploded, coming down hard with his right fist on the table.

"Are you sure?" she asked calmly, trying to bring the situation down a notch or two.

"*Sí*. My sources are completely reliable. I pay them a small fortune to be on top of things."

"Okay. So what are we going to do?"

He took a sip of his wine. He seemed to have calmed down a bit.

"You will take care of this puto, and you will receive five hundred thousand dollars in cash when you are done. And by the way," he paused, taking another sip of wine, "that also covers your services for the customs job at the airport.

"Bueno. When and where?"

"It will happen in Guadalajara. We have much competition in the state of Jalisco, particularly in the city. You will make it look like an act of retribution against us."

"Sale."

****

The flight to Guadalajara from Mexico City was short, about fifty minutes. As she only had a carry-on, she bypassed the luggage carousel and walked toward the exit signs of the terminal.

"Buenas tardes, señorita," said a federal police officer standing behind a table situated to the left.

"Buenas tardes, Oficial."

"¿Me permite revisar su maleta, por favor?"

"Claro que *sí*," said Aline as she hoisted her suitcase up for inspection.

"What is the purpose of your trip to Guadalajara?" he asked, looking through the contents of her carry-on.

"Business."

"And what business are you in?"

"Extracción de oro."

"Ah. Mining company."

"*Sí*."

"Que le vaya bien," he said, zipping up the bag.

"Gracias."

Outside, Aline put on her sunglasses and looked for the driver and car she had been assigned by Teniente. A navy blue BMW with tinted glass pulled up in front of her, and the driver stepped out.

"Buenas tardes, señorita. Soy Ricardo, a sus *órdenes*," said the driver, taking the carry-on from her hand and placing it into the trunk.

"Mucho gusto. Soy Aline."

Ricardo was on the short side, forty-something with wavy hair and green eyes. Pleasant. "So, is this your first time in Guadalajara, Aline?" he asked in English with a thick accent as they stood outside the car.

"Yes. Where did you learn to speak English?"

"At school, and then later I took classes in a Canadian company that I worked for."

"Really? A Canadian company? I come from Canada."

"Wow. Canada is beautiful," he said. "I would very much like to visit your country one day, but it's very cold, no?"

Aline smiled. "Only during the winter months. Actually, the summer is very hot, like Acapulco." He opened the back passenger door, and she got in. "Is the hotel far from the airport?"

"Not too far. Maybe thirty minutes. It's very nice."

The Hotel Riu Plaza was lavish, with open spaces and extravagant floral arrangements and bellhops in pressed uniforms at the ready. It had its own heliport and forty-four floors. The pinnacle rose above the top floor, making it the tallest building in the city and second tallest in Mexico.

"Buenas tardes, señorita," said the front desk clerk.

"Buenas tardes. I'd like to check in, please."

"Yes, of course. Do you have a reservation?"

"Yes," she said, handing him her phony ID and credit card, the ones she had previously received.

"*Sí*. Aquí está. You are on the forty-third floor, just under the top floor, señorita."

"Muchas gracias."

Arriving at her room, Aline studied the detailed layout of the floor plan that was stuck to the back of the door with Velcro—emergency exits, elevators, and stairwells. Stepping out into the hallway, she did a quick walk-around to familiarize herself with her surroundings. *No CCTV cameras,* she observed.

Returning to the room, she closed the door, fastening the extra security latch in place. The only indication that Teniente had given her of what was to happen was a message she received a couple of days prior to her arrival in Guadalajara: "Order room service at exactly 8:06 p.m." As she still had a few hours, she set her watch and curled up in bed for a nap.

Her alarm chimed at 7:15 p.m. Aline got up and took a shower. Changing into a pair of comfortable jeans and a plain, black T-shirt, she tied her hair back in a ponytail and didn't apply any makeup whatsoever. *No unnecessary attention, if possible.* She put on her running shoes and sat on the bed to tie the laces.

"Buenas noches, señorita," said a male voice on the other end of the phone at 8:06 p.m. "May I take your order?"

"*Sí*, por favor."

Twenty-five minutes later, there was a knock on the door.

"Room service."

Aline stepped toward the door and looked through the peephole. She unhooked the security latch and opened the door.

"Buenas noches," said a tanned, stocky guy in a hotel uniform and nametag. His shirt and pants were a bit tight for his thick frame. As he rolled the dinner trolley in, the hinged door swung closed behind him. "I have brought everything you will need, Aline. Before you leave the room, place your carry-on here." He indicated the empty space behind the aluminum doors of the cart. "I will pick it up when you are gone."

"Gracias," she said.

"You will receive a message on your cell phone when it is time."

"Okay."

"And when you are done, make your way directly to the heliport."

"Got it."

After closing the door behind the "waiter," she reviewed the contents of the trolley. Uncovering the first plate, she found a club sandwich. *Good idea,* she thought, taking a bite out of the snack while lifting the metal lid off the second plate. There lay a loaded Glock 26, 9mm pistol with threaded barrel, and next to it, a black, stainless-steel silencer.[65] *Baby Glock. Cute,* she thought, taking another nibble. Under the pistol was a hotel key card holder with one electronic card inside. Room 4213.

Aline finished her meal and tucked her carry-on into the cart. Tying her ponytail up into a bun, she covered her head with a tattered baseball cap and placed her dark, hooded jacket on the arm of one of the room's lounge chairs, sitting down comfortably. The jacket was light, a polyester, plain-weave fabric with adjustable draw cords that would easily conceal the pistol. Handling the diminutive Glock expertly, she attached the suppressor to the barrel and racked the slide, chambering the first round. Placing the pistol gently onto her lap, she closed her eyes and breathed deeply, playing out in her mind the scene to come.

At 9:01 p.m., her cell phone vibrated. An incoming text message from an unknown number:

Now.

Aline stood up calmly, placing the pistol behind her belt buckle, and put on the jacket, zipping it up partially. Key card in her right jeans pocket, she exited the room to the right, walking decisively to the nearest staircase. She opened the door and descended to the floor below, following the room number signs.

65 The term "silencer" could be more accurately replaced with the word "suppressor," as the noise emitted once the firearm is discharged is actually suppressed, not eliminated. This is often a semantic debate between enthusiasts. Both terms are acceptable.

4207...4209...4211...4213. Looking left and right, she made sure that the hallway was clear. Unzipping her jacket, she pulled the Glock out with her left hand and the key card with her right, placing it close to the reader above the door handle where a "Do Not Disturb" sign hung. *Green light*. She replaced the card in her right pocket, turned the handle with her sleeve-covered hand, and entered silently, pistol muzzle facing down at forty-five degrees.

Shower water running. Bathroom door slightly ajar. Room dimly lit. Alice in Chains song playing rather loudly—something about a rooster. She closed the door behind her gently, making no sound, and advanced cautiously into the room. Aline paused, stopping in her steps as she picked up a soft and familiar scent, trying to remember its origins. Clean and fresh, the fragrance filled her nostrils, and she briefly closed her eyes, swept up in a fleeting, almost pleasurable instant. Meanwhile, the water had turned off without her noticing.

Suddenly, in a moment of dreadful insight, she gasped, her right hand coming up to her mouth unconsciously, trying to smother the sound that had escaped through her lips. "Selene!" The bathroom door swung open briskly. Selene was standing there stark naked, water dripping down her body, pistol pointed at Aline.

No more than a couple of minutes after Aline had entered the room and closed the door had housekeeping come around the corner. A thick-set lady in her mid-forties with short, dark hair was pushing a cart full of tissue boxes, shampoo, and bath gels. Stopping at Room 4209 with a sign that read "Please Make Up

Room" on the door, she knocked, announcing herself, and entered. Leaving the door open, she returned to her cart, now aware of the music coming from Room 4213. Unwrapping a roll of toilet paper, she shrieked when she heard three muffled but distinct gunshots and a thud, like something hitting the floor. She dropped the roll and hurried frantically down the hallway to find her supervisor and inform hotel security.

Picking up the three casings, Aline replaced the Glock behind her belt and bolted for the door, grabbing the handle with her jacket sleeve, and ran for the stairwell from which she had come. Two stairs per stride, she scrambled upward. *Floor 43…44…Rooftop.*

Slamming into the door, she pushed it open and burst out onto the top of the building. A helicopter was waiting, ready to take off. Advancing quickly toward the chopper, she lowered her head instinctively as she passed under the main rotor blade and opened the door. The pilot, with headset on, didn't turn around to see her as she stepped up into the seat and closed the door. Speaking into the microphone boom, she couldn't hear what he was saying over the noise as they took off into the dark sky.

****

She sat at a local bar in Leon, Guanajuato watching the television news broadcast.

"This just in from Guadalajara, Jalisco," said the TV reporter. "Unidentified female slain in luxury hotel. Authorities are looking to anyone who may have information concerning the incident, which occurred this evening around 9:30 p.m. in the Hotel

Riu. Preliminary reports suggest it may be related to organized crime."

Aline emptied her glass with disdain and signed to the bartender to bring her another. *Hell of a night.*

CHAPTER 11

Tixtla, Guerrero, just after midday. The air-conditioning was on full in the pickup as Aline pulled into the parking lot of Teniente's strip club, per orders.

"I guess there's always someone looking for entertainment," she said, trying to find a spot in the crowded parking lot. As she unbuckled her seat belt, she leaned forward and reached under the driver's seat with her left hand, feeling for the .38 Super that she was now accustomed to carrying when in Guerrero. The pistol was there in a leather holster, attached to the underside of the seat in an improvised but effective manner. *Reassuring.* She removed the piece gently, placing it behind her belt at the back, and pulled her shirt over it before exiting the pickup.

Inside, the bar was dark, and there was no sense of time of day. Teniente was sitting at his usual table, and he waved to her when she came into view.

"¿Cómo estás, Aline?"

"Bien, gracias," she said, taking a seat.

"Buen trabajo en Guadalajara," he continued, placing his hand firmly on her forearm.

"It would have been good to know who the target was," she said somewhat agitatedly.

"Yes, but in this case I was not sure how you would react to the mark being Selene. Desgraciada perra," he blurted, his voice laced with malice. "Me vió la cara, but in the end, she got hers."

"It was her karma," said Aline softly, so much so that she had probably meant it for herself. But Teniente did not notice, as he was ordering another round.

"Well, on to bigger things," he said, leaning in a bit closer to speak in confidence. "You know, I have been observing El Líder for some time now, and I believe that he has become too comfortable and lazy in his position. Está de hueva," he emphasized. "Too many opportunities have gone by, and when there's some follow-up to be done, he brushes it off. I think it's time for a change in management."

"What do you have in mind?" she asked.

"I will have him removed and then take his place as the new head of the organization."

"It's not going to be easy. No direct line of attack head on. He's too well protected. You would most certainly lose many of your crew, and if you were unsuccessful, then it would give rise to another rival conflict."

"*Sí*. Tienes razón. So, what do you think? How would you take care of it?" he asked.

"Well, as I feel it would be very unlikely for him to become a victim of an act of God anytime soon, or stepping barefoot on an alacrán by accident, we need to instigate something that would appear totally circumstantial where there's little to no possibility that we would be even considered an influence."

"And what would that magical solution be?" he asked skeptically.

Looking him in the eye, she said, "Other than rival gangs, internal insurrections, the Army, PGR, and Federal Police, who's the number-one entity gunning for El Líder?"

"La Marina, of course," he replied.

"Exactly. The Navy has been systematically working toward dismantling the organization ever since they were given carte blanche to carry out operations nationwide."

"And what does that have to do with anything? What are we going to do? Call them up and ask them to dispose of El Líder?"

"Something like that."

****

"Frank, do you have a minute?" asked Aline, spotting the Risk & Intelligence manager coming out of the Information Gathering Center.

"Of course."

"Let's chat in my office. Would you like a coffee?" she asked.

"No thanks. Just finished my afternoon dose. So, what's up?"

"Regional Top Management has been receiving a lot of pressure from Corporate with respect to the security situation around the Guerrero mine, and subsequently, I have been receiving an earful from Woody and the director of Corporate Security."

"What do you want to do?"

"Well, since we have the IGC up and running and churning out intel reports like a production line, I think it's time we bump up our intelligence game. The biggest problem in Guerrero is not a lack of information concerning the bad guys but the inability to have that intel serve the purpose of dismantling the criminal groups."

"What do you mean?" asked Frank inquisitively.

"Do you recall the meeting we had with the Federal Police in Acapulco that I told you about, where the regional coordinator kept harping on the idea that the only way the criminals could be prosecuted would be after someone raised a legal claim against them?"

"Yeah, I remember. I'm sure that there are plenty of Guerrerenses waiting to line up at their local public ministry office to make official declarations as to who is extorting, kidnapping, and executing members of their communities," he said sarcastically.

"Right. We know that's just not gonna happen, so I was thinking, which government body is the most likely, and probably the quickest, to put some type of operation into effect based on received intelligence?"

"SEMAR?" interjected Frank, sitting up.[66]

"Yup. The Navy. If there's one group that is capable of sweeping through an area and taking out the trash, it's them."

"This is getting interesting."

"The premise is to funnel intel to the Navy concerning persons and movements in the region. Small tidbits of information will be transmitted to them via telephone from a diversity of anonymous informants during various times and days of the week and from different locations."

....

66 SEMAR—Short for *Secretaria de Marina*, which translates to Naval Secretary.

"Do you have a specific mark in mind?" asked Frank.

"Yes. El Líder."

"Wow. Trolling for big fish, are we?"

"I look at it this way. If he's taken care of, then I am sure that the current pressure on the mine will be alleviated, at least for a while."

"Makes sense, but as I understand it, he isn't seen too often around the mine. I have heard that on occasion he appears in Chilpancingo but that he most likely works out of Acapulco."

"That's true, but his organization definitely operates in the area, and I think that he handles matters through one of his deputies."

"So, what's my role?"

"I need you to call up your most reliable investigative contact to start putting together a short list of people, both men and women, who can mimic local accents and have been utilized previously."

"Okay."

"Meanwhile, I will prepare separate, concise information packages from the IGC regarding El Líder himself—vehicles, plates, movements, girlfriends, and frequented places, which will be delivered to your contact. The gist of the stratagem will be for each caller to know of and provide only a small, scripted part of the overall puzzle. As we know, all of the phone calls received by SEMAR are recorded and then sent to the corresponding investigative section for further processing. They will analyze the content, and in short time, one or more of their investigators will identify and extrapolate recurring commonalities from the information. Once that's done, they will synthesize the intel and disseminate it to their respective operative groups for execution."

"Me gusta," said Frank. "It seems that you have thought the whole thing through, down to the last detail."

"Yeah," replied Aline. *More than you can imagine.*

For the next few weeks, intel was systematically pumped into the SEMAR pipeline, with anonymous phone calls made by concerned citizens with information regarding El Líder's organization.

"Sí, señor," said an older man calling from Carrizalillo. "I have seen the same Audi, license plate GZX-24-09, two to three times in the last couple of days, and the men inside look like narcos, and they carry pistolas. My neighbors say that they are El Líder's men."

"No sé," answered a young single mother at a payphone in Chilpancingo the following morning. "I only know that the short, heavy man with a thick moustache has a lot of big guys around him, and he often goes to see a girl named Ana who lives behind the IMSS Clinic on Avenida Miguel Alemán."

Noticias Associated Press

Chilpancingo: Capo dies in clash with Navy

CHILPANCINGO DE LOS BRAVO (AP) – A *capo* from one of the dominant cartels in Guerrero was killed in a clash with the Mexican Navy, stated authorities late Friday. Through a public statement, the State Prosecutor's Office reported the death of *El Líder* during an armed

> confrontation with *los marinos* registered on Thursday evening in the city of Chilpancingo.
> The press release stressed that during the Naval campaign, different high-caliber weapons were seized, including a grenade launcher, in addition to tactical and radio communication equipment. According to a state official, who asked to remain anonymous, *El Líder* was directly linked to the deaths of a number of government officials and citizens and had a principal role in the movement of opium gum in the region.

"Lo lograste, cabrona," said Teniente, nodding his head in approval at Aline as they sat over a late lunch in a small restaurant situated near the famous cliff, La Quebrada, in Acapulco. The place was practically empty, except for a couple of local fishermen at a table outside, cooling off with *cervezas* and a local mutt dozing softly in the shade of the entrance.

"I don't know how, but you did it, and for this, I am making you my deputy, and tonight, I will present you as my right-hand man...lady," he corrected.

Aline sat back and smiled, enjoying her usual *mojito* and the warm sea breeze gently caressing her face. "How many of our people will be attending the meeting?" she asked.

"Perhaps eight to ten, depending on their availability, and a few friends and acquaintances. I would like for you to meet the heads of the different cells of our organization."

Aline awoke in darkness, close to 11:30 p.m. Sitting up in bed, she heard loud voices and laughter coming from somewhere downstairs. Rubbing the sleep from her eyes, she tried to gain her bearings and figure out where she was. She peered out of the open, second-story window that overlooked a small street. *Acapulco. La Quebrada.*

After a few drinks, she had decided to lie down and *echarse un coyote* before the evening's event. Teniente had directed her to a room upstairs with a single bed and a tiny bathroom. She washed her face, ran her fingers through her hair, and applied some lip gloss, puckering her mouth. "Not that bad," she said, looking at herself in the mirror.

Making her way down the steps, she spotted Teniente and walked toward him, passing a short and heavy, obnoxious-looking guy with his shirt open, holding a half-empty bottle of Don Julio in his right hand. "Looks like La Bella Durmiente is finally awake," he said tauntingly, giving her a light slap on the bum. Aline stopped cold a few feet from Teniente, her left fist clenching involuntarily.

"I would exercise caution with those kinds of words, mi estimado Pepe, unless you want her to romper tu hocico," laughed Teniente, not hiding his stern glance. Pepe's smirk quickly disappeared and was replaced with a notable paleness. Beads of sweat started to form spontaneously on his forehead.

"Discúlpame, Jefe, and you too, señorita," he said apologetically.

"Descuida," said Aline, smiling. Then she leaned in close to his right ear and whispered, "Next time, te parto la madre."

"Everyone, listen up," commanded Teniente. "I would like to present to you Miss Aline, mi segundo. As of this moment, she has all of the rights and privileges of the position, and in my absence, will have the final word on all matters. Let's give her a round of applause." The clapping was loud and long lasting.

"Congratulations, Señorita Aline," said an extraordinarily large man as he approached her, extending his thick hand for a handshake. "I am glad to finally make your acquaintance. Your reputation precedes you."

"Muchas gracias, señor."

"Call me Pitufo," he said, winking at her.

"Okay, mucho gusto," she replied...*Smurf,* she added silently.

"Can I get you a cold beer?" he asked.

"That would be great." Aline looked around the restaurant filled with bodies to see if she recognized anyone. There was an older couple sitting at a table that she identified from one of Teniente's previous parties and a girl in a tight skirt and top from the bar in Tixtla, flirtatiously rubbing the arm of a guy wearing a cowboy hat and checkered shirt.

"Man, is it hot in here," she said under her breath, deciding to step out for some air. The breeze was surprisingly cooler than she had expected. She walked for a few minutes in no particular direction, thinking about life and how things had unfolded. Reaching a low-standing stone wall that looked down to the ocean, she stopped, placed her hands on top of the barrier, and closed her eyes, breathing in the air contentedly. Hearing footsteps, she turned nimbly to see who was approaching. Pepe. The same bottle of tequila in hand, almost completely empty.

"Señorita Aline," he slurred, "buenas noches." *So much for a quiet, pleasant moment.*

"Buenas noches, Pepe," she said sharply.

"You know, I think we really got off on the wrong foot," he said, finishing the last drop of alcohol. "It must really feel good to have reached such a high post in Teniente's organization and to be such a pretty little thing, no less." He grinned.

Aline felt blood surging to her temples and noticed a change in her breathing pattern. "Mira, Pepe," she started, now noticeably annoyed. "I think you better go and sleep off the booze."

Oblivious to the imminent danger, Pepe moved in closer. "Listen. Don't get me wrong. I respect you. I just think that maybe we should get to know one another a little better," he continued, closing the distance between them even more. "What do you—"

Before he could finish the sentence, Aline coiled tightly and threw a powerful short left hook to his jaw, twisting his head to the side and ejecting two teeth from his gaping mouth while his body crumbled to the ground. Groggy, but still conscious, he turned his head and looked up at her with a bloodied mouth.

"Eres una per—"

Once again, Pepe was cut off, this time as Aline's steel-toed *Berrendo* came down hard onto his skull, knocking him senseless.

"Idiota," she said, turning and walking back to the restaurant.

****

"Morning. How was your weekend?" asked Frank, passing by Aline's open door, Vespa helmet in one hand while searching his pockets for the keys to his office with the other.

"Quiet," she said. "How about yours?"

"Fine. You know, go-karts and family stuff."

"That's nice."

"What's on the agenda today?" he inquired.

"There's a new Company initiative that we were informed about concerning sustainability and excellence. Why don't you grab a coffee and bring it in here and we can start to chat about the system. When Lewis gets in, he can join us."

"Okay."

"By the way, did you see the last closing price for gold?" he asked.

"Sure did. Pretty brutal. USD $1,190 per ounce."

"It's downright scary, if you ask me, and if it keeps nose-diving, I'm sure we will see more than just the suspension of projects and changes in Regional Management."

"Unfortunately, I am convinced of that, amigo mío," said Aline forebodingly.

CHAPTER 12

It was after dark in a hotel lounge in Chilpancingo. "Salud," said Teniente, tapping his glass softly against Aline's.

"Salud," she replied, taking a sip of her champagne. She was dressed to kill in a sleek cocktail dress and heels, with hair, makeup, and nails done. Teniente looked her over, then leaned in and said, "Who would imagine that someone who looked like an angel was really in league with El Diablo."

"Gracias." *I think.* "So, what's the celebration this evening?" she asked.

"New opportunities," he answered, smiling.

"Like what?"

"Do you remember when I told you that El Líder was letting potential prospects go by?"

"Yes, I do."

"Well, there's one right in front of us that no one seems to have pursued until now."

"And what would that be?"

"The Company's mine in Guerrero."

Aline stifled a gasp, bringing her glass up to her mouth quickly, attempting to conceal the tightness in her lips and make it look like what he had said did not affect her.

"I can see that this bothers you, no?"

"No, not really," she said calmly, thinking rapidly about what she was going to say next. "It's just that I know for a fact that the Company has had several meetings with government officials, and rumor has it that they have contact with the military zone in the area, which I am sure would cause us problems if we were to force something."

"That could very well be. Nevertheless, I think I have a solution to that little inconvenience."

"And what would that be?"

"You."

"What do you mean?" she asked, genuinely dumbfounded.

"Yes, you. Aline Jean Belanger. Regional Director of Security for the Company. At least, that's what it says on LinkedIn," he said brashly. *Well, there goes my maintenance façade,* she thought.

"And when did you find out about me?"

"To be honest with you," he said, emptying the rest of the champagne bottle into his glass, "I knew right from the start. I needed precisely you in my organization, the only person in the Company within the region on a high-enough level who was involved in all corporate dealings and who also had insider information with respect to how the gold was guarded.

"So what do we do now?" she asked resolutely.

"Nothing. We stick to my plan. Come on, let's face it. You have it a lot better working for me. Don't tell me that you haven't enjoyed yourself. Besides, there is the matter of you being linked with two homicides and making sure that a shipment of heroin got to the U.S., not to mention your costly little habit." He wiped his nose allegorically.

"Okay, so it's pretty clear. What's next?"

"As you are very apt at organizing and carrying out sophisticated plans, you will orchestrate how my men and I will enter and then exit the mine with the gold. If you do a good job, no one will have to get hurt, right?"

"Yeah. I'll take care of it."

****

The Plan.

"Nice quandary you got yourself into, Aline," she said to herself, going over the layouts of the mine and the airfield with a pencil behind her ear. "If it was all easy, then you'd be bored, right? Too much chatter. Back to the drawing table."

She pulled out blueprints for the refinery, then browsed over the mine's timetable for the next shipments of doré to be carried out. Too complicated to explain the difference to Teniente, between the shiny gold bars he's seen in the movies and what the mine actually produced. Anyway, he should be content enough with the value of the doré bars. Besides, at least these bars were only twenty to twenty-five kilograms apiece and much easier to move around, not like the stuff coming out of the Zacatecas mine.

Aline picked up a marker and highlighted a day on the schedule. "Looks like the last Friday of the month is the day of choice. Biggest accumulation of doré to be shipped out for the period and the least amount of employees on-site. It also coincides nicely with a legal holiday, which means that the majority of people will take Thursday off as well.

"Management would be off-site," she contemplated, "and security would be in the hands of the 2 I/C. Just need to get him to attend something out of the mine." She drank from her bottle of water and looked around her dining room. "Think. How's this gonna pan out? It's gotta be fast, with little effort, limited to no casualties, and a good dose of misdirection to boot. The fast part is easy—plane in and out. Dash 8 ought to do it. Bigger cargo hold, and it can fly a hell of a lot faster and farther than the other planes. Little effort. Hmm. Don't want to be hiring power lifters to move the bars, so let's get the doré to come to us—to the plane to be precise. Besides, if I send the lifters to the refinery, there would be a lot of movement and way too much security to bypass, and no doubt we would lose some of the guys on the way there or back to the airstrip. Seven chaps should be just about right. And finally, the misdirection. It needs to be something big, but not too big. Just enough to get attention without causing the whole region to go ballistic."

She twirled the pencil in her right hand, imagining this and that. "Unscheduled detonations in the open pit. Still have access to the Tovex 100 that was found a while back. Should be enough to have people at the mine trying to figure out what was happening in the pit while the shipment left the premises as usual."

****

She dialed Teniente from her cell.

"Hola. ¿Cómo estás?" she asked Teniente.

"Bien. ¿Y tú? How are things progressing?"

"Fine. When can I see you?"

"How about tomorrow night, same place?"

"Okay."

"I'll be waiting for you."

The drive to Chilpancingo was monotonous, but at least there were no *retenes*. She parked her vehicle and entered the bar.

"Buenas noches, señorita," said Teniente politely.

"Hola," she replied curtly.

"Something to drink?"

"Cerveza, por favor."

"Please sit. I am very eager to hear your master plan. Why don't you tell me about it?" Aline began to explain the schematic for the Friday in question in great detail, only stopping from time to time to answer Teniente's questions.

"So, what is my role and that of my men?"

"All of you will be miners returning to work after a few days of rest. I will get everyone Company IDs. Just send me the photos. The standard safety gear—vests, hard hats, and boots—can be picked up at any local shop in Mezcala or Carrizalillo."

"*Órale*."

"Once the plane lands, your men will pick up their gear from the cargo hold, then walk casually to the security check-in. You will stay onboard to make sure that the pilot doesn't cause any trouble. I don't think he's going to be too cooperative, so you will have to be leaning on him from start to finish."

"Oh, you don't have to worry about him."

"Why's that?"

"Because he is my cousin on my mother's side and has been receiving a nice salary from me for some time now. You know, for special services."

"Fine. Then just make sure that he takes care of two items. The first is to ensure that only the seven of you are allowed on the flight. As per his usual duties, he will check your identifications and tick off your names on his passenger list to make everything look normal. As I have already reviewed the Human Resources list for that day, there is no one scheduled for the early flight. On the off chance that someone does appear, the pilot will inform the person that the aircraft is loaded to capacity with cargo and equipment, and only the seven registered passengers will be permitted to fly, of course reassuring them that they can take the next available flight."

"Bien. And the second point?"

"He has to get your guys' weapons onto the plane at the hangars in Cuernavaca."

"Nothing new there," he said.

"Good. And even though you don't have to watch the pilot anymore, I still need you to stay out of sight on the aircraft so we don't change the other parts of the plan."

"Got it."

"There are only two armed Federal Protection agents stationed at the airfield, one making rounds along the outer perimeter and the other at the guardhouse. There will also be an unarmed auxiliary police officer sitting at a table in front of the small building registering all passengers. Your people will have to be carrying, but only concealed pistols at this point. Once inside the guardhouse, three of them will overpower the Federal Protection agent and gag him and tie him up, but not before they take his uniform off. Two will subdue the unarmed officer, also taking his uniform. And the last guy will be solely responsible for monitoring the other agent making the rounds. When the first agent and the officer have been restrained, they need to be placed in the locker room located to the right as you step into the building, while two of your fellows will be tasked with putting on the Federal Protection and auxiliary police uniforms, respectively. Is that clear so far?"

"*Sí.*"

"Okay. As soon as they have changed into the uniforms, your new FP agent will very calmly signal to the agent patrolling along the fence to come to the guardhouse."

"But won't the agent see that it isn't his colleague when he gets closer to the building?"

"Very unlikely. At this time of year, there is so much dust and dirt on the airstrip due to wind conditions that visibility is quite poor. All of the agents will be wearing helmets, balaclavas, and dark goggles. When the patrolling agent enters the building, they will have to overpower him as well, then take his uniform, and repeat the same steps as before. After gaining control of the guardhouse, your three remaining miners will return to the plane and prepare their assault rifles. Three AK-47s will do, as the real agents who will be escorting the doré from the refinery to the airfield will only be carrying Mendoza .380 caliber, semiautomatic sub-machine guns and pistols. There will be four of them, plus one from the Company's Security Department, who will be me."

"¿Qué? How will you be able to get into the operation?" asked Teniente, perplexed.

"Well, as the 2 I/C—in this case the coronel—will be called off for an unexpected family urgency, I will gladly step in to cover, as it will happen that I will be on-site from the day before. The security contingency will have one driver, who will always remain in the truck, and three escorts. The truck will approach the airstrip, and the driver will confirm with the agent at the gate whether all is clear. Once he receives the go-ahead, the vehicle will pull up to the plane's hold while the aircraft will already be aligned with the runway, ready to taxi. As per protocol, the agent who was at the gate—now your guy—will make his way to the plane to supervise the operation while two agents from the truck will start unloading the bars in order to load them onto the aircraft. The pilot, as normal practice, will have opened the cargo hold and will be standing close by until the loading is complete so that he can then close and latch the door. Meanwhile, the agent who is sitting in the passenger seat will get out and board the plane to check that everything is okay. Your three guys onboard will be waiting to receive him. When he is disarmed and under control, you will make sure that he stays that way, and the three will storm off the plane with the assault rifles, two pointing at the agents occupied with the doré, and the third with sights on the driver. This third guy will demand that the driver throw his pistol out of the window, and he will then order me to get out of the truck and board the aircraft as a hostage. All the while, your man from the gate will be covering with his pistol. As soon as the bars are loaded, your guys on the ground near the plane will join us onboard, and we fly off, having them first remove the FP agent. Your two guys at the guardhouse will take the Federal Protection pickup and drive off toward Chilpancingo. I would suggest that they dump the truck en route and have another vehicle pick them up."

"And how can we be sure that no one from the mine, like Security, will decide to make rounds close to the airfield precisely when the cargo is being loaded?"

"Ah. That's where the misdirection comes in. We will have a set of explosions go off in the open pit when I send the signal, just about halfway through the loading of the doré, which will be immediately reported to Security, who will investigate what is happening, taking them even further away from us."

Teniente made a show of slow and purposeful clapping. "Eres chingona, Aline. Me gusta," he exclaimed.

"There are only two more things to consider. One is the hour. The movement is scheduled to take place a little after dawn. 6:24 a.m. to be exact. I already checked the official prognostic for that Friday."

"Bien. And the other?"

"I need to find someone to set the sequence for the detonations in the open pit."

Teniente smiled. "Again, no worries. One of my nephews is part of the underground mine, and he works with explosives."

"Well, I guess we're set then."

CHAPTER 13

Sunrise over mine,
Dark shadows fall onto light,
Seraphim align.

Friday morning, just after dawn.

"Buenos días, Aline," said the coronel. "How did you sleep?"

"Very well, thanks."

"I can see that something's on your mind. What's up?"

"I just received a call that my mother is in the hospital, and I need to go to Mexico City."

"Yes, of course. You should leave immediately."

"But the problem is that I'm leading the contingency for today's doré movement."

"No worries there. I can step in to cover you."

"Muchas gracias. I will have the gear sent to your room."

"I also think it's best that a Federal Protection agent drives you. That way you don't have to have the additional task of driving yourself."

"Gracias."

The escort team rendezvoused in front of the security office, with the fortified pickup ready to go.

"Okay, listen up," said Aline. As the coronel mentioned, I will be covering his role on the team. Any questions?"

"Ninguna. Nada," replied the Federal Protection agents.

"Bien. Let's go to the refinery."

Beep. Beep. Beep. The driver put the pickup in reverse confidently, backing up toward the cargo doors of the refinery. The doors of the building swung open, and two guards walked out, unlatching the tailgate of the truck. The FP agents got out and took their positions partially inside the area, with sub-machine guns locked and loaded while the driver stayed behind the wheel. Aline supervised the loading of each doré bar, individually wrapped in a small but sturdy, thick, grey canvas bag with a drawstring and corresponding numbered metal seal. Twenty-five bars in total. *Nice,* she thought.

"All right, let's move out."

"Buenos días," said the driver to the Federal Protection agent at the gate to the airfield.

"Buenos días."

"¿Alguna novedad?"

"No, nothing to report at the moment," he said, opening the gate. The driver nodded. The truck slowly edged forward, then picked up speed, heading toward the plane. The driver came to a complete stop at the orange cones that marked the outer perimeter for the plane, which no vehicle was permitted to cross. Three of the FP agents got out, while Aline and the driver stayed in the truck. The first agent looked around the plane, while the other two went to the back of the pickup and started to unload the doré.

"Buenos días, Capi" said the first agent, extending his hand to the pilot.

"Buenos días. ¿Como te va?" he asked.

"Bien. I'm just going to check that everything is okay onboard."

"Claro. Adelante," he replied. The agent grabbed the handrail and climbed the steps to the aircraft. Because there was so much noise from the constant wind and the plane's engine, no one could hear the scuffle that was taking place in the aircraft or the thud of the agent as he was cold-cocked. The other two continued with their laborious task of unloading and loading the bars, while Aline discreetly sent a message to Teniente's nephew, who was in the open pit.

"Bajen las armas, cabrones," ordered one of the "agents" menacingly, racing down the steps from the plane, already pointing his AK-47 at the totally astounded Federal Protection agents near the cargo hold. As he approached them, the two other "agents" had already made it to the ground, one joining his companion, and the other pointing his weapon at the driver.

"No te muevas, puto," he said. "Throw your pistol out the window and leave your hands on the steering wheel where I can see them."

Be still, and know that I am, said a voice in Aline's head as she closed her eyes for a moment. She breathed deeply, visualizing the game plan.

"You in the back seat. Get out of the truck slowly," demanded the "agent." Aline opened the left-side door of the double cabin, and with hands raised slightly, got out of the vehicle. "We're going on a little trip," he said, moving her forward with his assault rifle. As they passed in front of the pickup, the driver very subtly looked to the right to determine the exact position of Teniente's guy, who had come up from the gate and was watching the loading process.

"Oye," yelled the driver at the agent about a meter behind Aline, having stepped out of the pickup imperceptibly in the lapse of a few seconds. As the agent turned and raised his weapon, the driver fired two rounds at him, then aimed to the right and shot the other agent standing nearby. At the exact instant that Aline heard *"oye"* she deholstered her sidearm on the left side and, taking quick aim at Teniente's startled men, fired. *Bang bang. Bang bang.* Two double taps, dropping both of them.

Aline adjusted her sights on the incredulous pilot, who fumbled desperately for his gun tucked at the back, and shot him dead before he could reach it, sending his limp body to the dusty ground. The two FP agents who were loading the bars were lying face down, having instinctively taken cover after the first volley of shots from the driver. At a distance, two distinct and loud discharges could be heard coming from somewhere in the direction of the gate.

"Teniente!" roared Aline, peeling off her goggles and balaclava swiftly as she walked toward the steps of the plane, her pistol pointed at the entrance. "Teniente!" The driver approached Aline from the left, also removing the cumbersome eye protection and cloth headgear.

Teniente stepped into the opening with his pistol drawn on Aline, then stopped and stood there in utter disbelief at the sight before him. "Selene! But how? It's impossible," he stuttered, trying to maintain his composure. He looked back at Aline, his expression changing to wrath.

"Pinches viejas!" he seethed. "Me chingaron las dos!"

"Teniente," said Aline in a firm and commanding tone, "you are under arrest for multiple counts of murder and drug trafficking."

"Ha. Now that's what I call ironic, señorita. And what about you, princesa?" he said, looking at Selene. "What do you have to say for yourself?"

"Nada," she said, still pointing her gun at him alongside Aline. "Well, maybe just one thing. Pendejo eres y siempre serás."

"Bueno. Enough of this insipid banter. So, what happens next?" he asked mockingly.

"Let's see," said Aline. "You could come down here, hand over your gold-plated .38 Super, and we take you into the Attorney General's Office nice and easy—"

"Nah. I'm definitely not liking that idea too much," he interjected.

"Or we could chat for a bit longer until I get bored, then I shoot you down like the dirty dog that you are."

"Hmm. No, not into that one either."

"Well, then I guess we're at a bit of an impasse."

"Not really," he said. "I think it's time to address this situation, con los huevos puestos," he said, aiming at Aline with precision.

"Your call, amigo." Teniente looked at them both, trying to anticipate whom he would be able to kill first, and with any luck, hit the second one, on his way down.

Time seemed to stand still, if not having stopped altogether. Aline was breathing rapidly but steadily, her senses heightened, only cueing in to the most relevant information in her environment, while filtering out the rest. Selene's breathing was short and quick. Her right index finger was no longer straight along the side of her pistol but was instead wrapped lightly around the trigger, waiting to discharge. Teniente's gaze was fixed and his body tense, with beads of sweat running down the sides of his face.

Then something unexpected happened. The wind ceased without warning, and a dead calm ensued. Out of nowhere, a soft, cool breeze, swept across their faces, quieting everything ubiquitously, as if some omniscient force was making a last-ditch effort to bring about peace. Teniente brought his arms down to his sides, as if lulled into a trance, with Selene following suit. Aline resisted futilely, lowering her pistol, but she still held the weapon with both hands. A dreamlike fog had encroached on their minds, dulling out sound and sight. No thoughts or movements, only motionless tranquility, a cosmic time-out of sorts.

But then, as quickly as the phenomenon had appeared, so too did it diminish. Teniente awoke, looking up at Aline, rage filling his eyes once more.

"See you in Hell, perra!" he screamed, raising his pistol as Aline emptied her magazine into his body.

"Been there and back."

EPILOGUE

JTF Meeting—CSIS HQ, Ottawa, Canada.[67] Eight months prior to joining the Company.

"Ladies and Gentlemen. Thank you for your interest and participation in this joint effort to thwart shared threats to our nation and to Mexico," said the agency executive, Mr. Bloom, Director of the Canadian Security Intelligence Service. Aline looked around the table at the seven-member Canadian Task Force, made up of five men and two women.

"Your counterparts in Mexico are six senior agents from the PGR specifically tasked with this transnational collaboration.[68] Together, the cryptonym for this Canadian-Mexican Team will be SERAPHIM. As per your team leader, each of you has been assigned to a predetermined detail according to your profile and skill sets. Once you are implanted into your particular assignment, there will be absolutely zero contact with the Agency or with the rest of the Canadian contingent. In addition, you will not be presented to your Mexican colleagues, and neither part will have any knowledge

....

67 Joint Task Force Meeting—CSIS—Canadian Security Intelligence Service.

68 PGR—Attorney General's Office, Mexico.

of the other members with respect to what they are working on. In the unlikely event that your paths cross or a situation presents itself where there is no alternative whatsoever, the Task Force code word is ANGEL. Thank you again, and good luck."

The group got up and headed out the door. Walking to the coffee machine, the team leader caught up with Aline.

"So, what do you think?" he asked.

"Pretty good, at all of about five minutes in length," she joked. "And the clincher was the director's subtle message of all of us being alone and shit outta luck if anything goes down. You gotta love this job," she added, letting out a laugh.

"Well, you're the only one that got a double-implant task," he told her.

"Yeah, that part is cool."

"Do you have any idea of how to get into the Company?" he asked.

"Yes, I do. I have a really good contact in the automotive industry who works at a German automaker. This guy knows pretty much everyone and their brother. I'll start bitching about my current job, and one way or another, establish contact through him with one of the corporate headhunters that the Company uses and make my way in."

"And Teniente's group? You know, we are betting on the idea that he will be the one who takes charge of the cartel."

"Already working on it," she replied.

****

Hotel Plaza Riu. Encounter, Room 4213.

The bathroom door swung open briskly. Selene was standing there stark naked, water dripping down her body, pistol pointed at Aline.

"Puta Madre! ¿Qué haces aquí, cabrona?" exclaimed Selene.

"Killing you apparently," replied Aline.

"I guess it's pretty clear that my cover has been blown," laughed Selene.

"You think?" snickered Aline, lowering her firearm.

Selene paused for a moment, looking at her purposefully. "Does the word 'angel' mean anything to you?"

"No chinges!" cried Aline, completely bewildered. "Well, it's nice to meet you, Señorita PGR."

"Likewise, Ms. CSIS."

"Okay, down to business. Your crew has to clean this up fast. I only have a few minutes before I need to be on the rooftop," said Aline, placing a thick pillow against the bed frame and taking aim with the Glock.

"Nice piece," observed Selene.

"Yeah. I'm going to fire off three rounds. You pick up the chair and time it after the third discharge. One. Two. Three." Three consecutive gunshots and a thud.

"Nos vemos, chica," said Selene.

"Vaya con Dios," said Aline. Picking up the three casings, Aline replaced the Glock behind her belt and bolted for the door.

****

The Other Plan.

"So, do you think that he bought it?" asked Selene, delicately wiping the moist condensation off the side of the plastic cup of iced mocha with her right index finger.

"Hook, line, and sinker," answered Aline.

"That arrogant son-of-a-bitch. He really thought that he was the one who selected you all along?"

"Yup."

"Well, he's gonna get his," said Selene.

"And then some."

"I hope I get a chance to see his face when it happens."

"I'm pretty sure you will," Aline said smiling cunningly.

"Okay. So, I understand the plan that you explained to Teniente. Now, how do I fit into this one?"

"I will get you on-site Thursday evening with Company ID and an altered document, stating that you are a new member from the Corporate Security team in Vancouver that is on a regional tour with me. When the coronel asks why you look and sound like a Mexican, you will smile and say that you were born in Canada to Mexican parents and grew up in a Latino community."

"That sounds pretty believable."

"For sure, and with your smile and flirty attitude, you will have him eating out of your hand."

"You can count on that," she said, giggling. "I will also get you a disposable cell phone and the coronel's number. Around 5:30 a.m. you will call him with a slight change of voice, saying you are the neighbor of his mother in Mexico City and that she was taken to the hospital and requested that you call him. You will have to stress that his mother is asking to see him urgently. When he comes to me with a concerned face, and I ask him about what is going on, he will tell me, and I will insist that he leave immediately, and that it would be better if one of the Federal Protection agents drives him. Once he's off-site, we will gear-up—balaclavas and all—and make our way to the security office to liaise with the escorts. As the highest ranking Company security person presently at the mine, I will have the final word with respect to the entire doré movement. I will then give you the task of driver of the reinforced pickup. Please remember that every time you put the truck in reverse, you will need to beep the horn three times in a row."

"Beep the horn three times when putting truck in reverse," she jotted down in her notebook.

"When the bars are loaded onto the bed of the pickup and we are all onboard, you will hit the horn twice, and then we make our way to the airfield. I will instruct the FP agent beside you to orient you to the route. Once we get to the gate, you will ask Teniente's guy in Federal Protection wear if everything is all right, and he will obviously say yes. You will then drive the truck toward the plane. As the real FP agent who has the responsibility of boarding the plane will be sitting in the front passenger seat, I will be in the back with the other two agents, who will be in charge of physically moving the doré."

"Okay."

"You and I will stay in the vehicle. Once the agents leave the pickup, I will send a message to Teniente's nephew to detonate the explosives in the open pit. As I mentioned before, when the agent that boarded the aircraft is controlled, three of Teniente's men will bolt off the plane with their assault rifles, two focused on the agents loading the bars and one pointing his weapon at you. He will order you to throw out your pistol, which you will do. I will ensure that you have another gun as a replacement, loaded and ready to fire. Per the plan, he will demand that I step out of the vehicle, at which point I will begin to walk slowly toward the others, with him in tow. You, with gun at the ready, will open the door, using it as cover, and simultaneously step out, yelling '*Oye*' at the guy, which will oblige him to turn toward you, his weapon already drawn. You will then take him out, and in the same movement, pivoting slightly to your right, you'll neutralize the other guy who came from the main gate. By that time, I will have used your verbal cue as my signal to deholster my pistol and double tap both of Teniente's men covering the agents and the pilot, who will be close to the cargo door."

"What about the two at the gate? We don't want to get clocked from behind."

"For sure. That's why I need you to establish contact with your team leader from the PGR and have two of your colleagues from the Task Force help us—one driver and one sniper with a .50 caliber Barrett rifle. They also need to acquire federal police uniforms and an official pickup truck."

"That shouldn't be too difficult. The PGR and Federal Police often collaborate in terms of operations."

"That's what I figured. The sniper will position himself on a well-concealed knoll located approximately two hundred and fifty meters away that is perfectly in line with the gate to the airstrip. I know it very well since the area was used as a military checkpoint about six months back and was later used by the Federal Police. It's camouflaged and very difficult to make out, even with binoculars. Your team members should be monitoring the situation from the beginning. As soon as the firefight starts, that's the signal for the sniper to go loud."

"Perfect."

"Once Teniente's ground crew is neutralized, I will order him out of the plane and inform him that he is under arrest."

"Couldn't Teniente use the real Federal Protection agent that will still be tied up onboard as a hostage?"

"He could. However, if that happens, we'll have to deal with it. The idea is to bring Teniente in and have him processed by the Attorney General's Office."

****

A little take on good and evil.

> There is light in the darkness, as there is darkness in the light; not one truly separated from the other.
>
> The Dark One. Lucifer, First of the Fallen, ever-present. Always seducing. Always ensnaring.
>
> But there is hope in the Light.
> The Once Fallen can rise anew.
> Forgiveness bestowed if atonement embraced, and Angels in Grace can banish the Serpent to the Abyss from whence it came.

A. J. BEHUL

A.J. Behul is an author and security expert with over two decades of experience in the industry on both the corporate and operational level. His work has taken him across North America and Europe and to countries like China and Mexico, where he was the head of security for three transnational corporations. He holds a bachelor's degree in political science and an executive master's degree in business administration. A.J. is a certified Use of Force instructor and is proficient in several forms of martial arts, having trained and fought in mixed martial arts, kickboxing, and full contact. He was, and is, the only person to hold the title of Regional Director of Security, for an organization that was both Mexico's principal gold producer and the world's largest gold mining company. A native of Canada, he speaks several languages, including English, Spanish, Slovak, and German, and has called Mexico home, for close to twenty years.

www.ingramcontent.com/pod-product-compliance
Lightning Source LLC
Chambersburg PA
CBHW070608310726
48982CB00001B/14